MW01139190

A
Game of
Catch

Published 2014.

ISBN-13: 978-1500481056

ISBN-10: 150048105X

A GAME OF CATCH

Proal Heartwell

In memory of my father, a great storyteller

I am indebted to many people for their help in the production of this book. Thanks to Kathryn Caine for her beautiful cover illustration. I am grateful for the help of Laura Roseberry for her cover design and for rescuing and formatting the text of A Game of Catch. *Finally, many thanks to Will McDavid for his editorial help and for his skills preparing the manuscript for publication.*

Contents

1963

Will

I'd like to be able to tell you that the day I first saw Joe was, in some way, extraordinary. But, in truth, the day we met, or the day I at least became conscious of his existence, was a day undistinguished by anything unusual. It was late August, a few weeks before school began or was scheduled to begin, the actual opening date to be determined by the demands of the tobacco crop on the children of the family-owned and operated farms of the county. That August morning would have found me restless. The youngest of three children, my siblings would have already left the house for their summer jobs, my brother laying asphalt with the highway department and my sister clerking at Bloom Brothers' Department Store; its manager, Izzy Cohen, couldn't pay her much after all, but he respected my family enough to do what he could.

For me, the highlight of those summer days was always baseball but we did not convene until after lunch in that most of my friends, because of family circumstances, did not have the luxury of idle time. Junior Thomas, in fact, would have gone with his father at six a.m. to open his place of business, The Little Store, a crossroads convenience market on the edge of town. Junior would begin his day sweeping the dusty wooden floors, stacking crates of empty soda bottles, and replenishing the drink cooler with 6½ oz. Coca-Colas. At noon, his father, remembering what it was to be a boy on a summer's day, would dismiss him to go home to lunch and then to my house for our afternoon game. Marvin Freeman would have been cutting grass since eight, or at least since the dew of the evening before had evaporated. Every week, Marvin mowed twelve lawns at two dollars each—$2.50 for Mr. Clary's sloping acre—and dutifully turned his money over to his mother who returned a dollar to him for his efforts.

I, on the other hand, might have spent a desultory morning hour picking pebbles from our home's expansive backyard, our makeshift diamond. More likely I would have despaired of this task after only a few minutes and resigned myself to the existence of the rocks, an irrefutable and tangible fixture in our daily game as evidenced by the many bad-hop bruises on our shins and chests.

But on that day I first saw Joe, with the achingly slow hours of morning ahead of me, I left my house about 10 a. m. on another of my ritual excursions downtown. It was a familiar route, a short walk down Windsor Avenue past my grandmother's house and the homes of various spinsters who taught at Robert E. Lee Elementary School; then by the gates of St. George's College and Emmanuel Episcopal Church, a small, white clapboard building responsible for my spiritual instruction. At the intersection of Church Street, I'd turn left, cross the road and cut across the lawn of the Methodist Church. It was a short trip from the back of the Church lot up the alley behind Bailey's Hardware Store to Main Street and the town square.

"Don't slam the door!" my mother automatically shouted as I left the house that morning. Still, I flung open the screen and launched myself across the porch. Three giant steps carried me across the front lawn to the sidewalk of Windsor Avenue. Clean cement, not yet yellowed by age and shuffling feet, surrounded the new grated opening of the subterranean water line. I had hastily scratched "D. M. & W. R." into the sidewalk the day before, moments after Ollie Poytress and Raymond Brewer, the town's ubiquitous utility men had replaced the cracked lid and surrounding cement. I looked up the sidewalk, hoping to see Dean escape from her house, but I knew that she was in the midst of her piano lesson, her one concession to her mother's insistence that she was a girl and could not defy the immutable laws of biology forever. Never mind that Dean was the best shortstop in the memory of two generations of males of Windsor Avenue.

I turned left and took twenty strides before my foot hit a crack in the sidewalk. I noticed the cars parked outside my grandmother's white-columned house. The ladies of the bridge club—June Nelson, Sue Bolling, and Helen Markley, Dean's grandmother—had gathered for cards. ("Or sherry," I thought.) I reminded myself to stop there on the way home for leftover nuts and mints. Across the street was the modest home of Miss Elfie and Miss Julia Lee, sisters who had not only taught me, my brother and sister, but my father as well at Robert E. Lee Elementary. These ladies demanded respect and I understood perfectly why my father, even at age 45, quickly extinguished his cigarette before walking by the sisters' home. I admired these ladies and it was with pride that at the conclusion of the previous school year, my sixth, I had given Miss Julia Lee my cherished silver dollar minted in 1895, the year of her birth.

Further down the street, I passed the pillared entrance to St. George's College, a small, all-black institution of teacher training and vocational skills. St. George's was affiliated with and sustained by the Episcopal Church and our diocese was instrumental in its administration. The 400 students of St. George's rarely strayed beyond the confines of the campus and its handful of teachers were unknown to the white community, excepting the town's merchants, like my father. My excursions to St. George's were rare—an occasional game of tennis on the only court in town and then, only in summer when school was not in session; or, on crisp fall afternoons accompanied by my father, to witness the Dragons valiantly engage some equally undermanned squad of football players from a like institution of the Southern Negro Collegiate League. These trips would always begin with my father asking, 'Did I ever tell you the story of 'Morning Morning' Jones?'" and despite my insistence that he had, many times, he embarked on the narrative once again.

"'Morning Morning' Jones wasn't always called 'Morning Morning.' No, he was born William Jones, son of William Jones who sharecropped a little piece of the Harrison's land out in the southern part of the county. Now, there was nothing to really distinguish young William Jones from any other colored boy except his ability to kick a football—to kick it barefoot, as a matter of fact. Yes, barefoot. And, of course, the other thing that marked him as 'unusual,' if you will, was that his standard reply to any query was, 'Morning Morning.' When he was a teenager, he'd come into town in his father's battered old pickup to fetch some feed at the store or some little notion or whatever for his mother, and no matter what you'd say to him, he would inevitably answer, 'Morning Morning.'

'How's your mother, William?'

'Morning Morning.'

'Nice day today, William.'

'Morning Morning.'

"And he would never look at you either. Just stare at the ground and scurry off at the first pause in the conversation, if you could call it that. Well, it didn't take long for the folks in town to just start calling William, 'Morning Morning.' And pretty soon whenever anyone would see him on the street, they would greet him with, 'Morning Morning, 'Morning Morning.' And of course he would reply, without lifting his head, 'Morning Morning."

Here Father would always laugh expectantly to make sure I understood the joke and I would smile out of courtesy.

"Well, anyway, as I said, 'Morning Morning' could really kick a football and you can bet that it didn't take long for Henry Solomon, the coach at St. George's, to get wind of this fact. He enrolled 'Morning Morning' at the college, never mind that he had not, as far as anyone could ascertain, gone to school past the sixth grade. Of course, 'Morning Morning' lasted only one semester but that was long enough to help the Dragons win the SNCL championship in 1949, the only year they accomplished that feat.

"Henry's plan was simple. Any time he got the ball in his opponent's half of the field, he'd line up for a field goal. It didn't matter what down it was or how much time was left in the half, Henry knew that bad things could happen when you tried to hold onto the ball. His own stingy defense had proven that to him and the other coaches around the league. So whenever the Dragons crossed the fifty-yard line, out hobbled 'Morning Morning', one shoe on and one shoe off, take one look at the goal posts and, at the snap and placement of the ball, swing his bare toes to the leather and split the uprights every time. It was amazing, it really was.

"Of course Henry would never let him kick off and run the risk of injuring himself on a tackle. No, 'Morning Morning' was a specialist, pure and simple. One of the first, I reckon. Well, of course, it couldn't last and after the first semester grades came out, 'Morning Morning' went back to helping his Daddy work that worn-out piece of land. And he's still working it today."

And with the conclusion of the tale, we'd be off to the game, during which my father would lament that they didn't make players like "Morning Morning" Jones or "Useful" Baker any more. But "Useful" Baker is another story.

A few short steps beyond the entrance to St. George's lay the intersection of Church Street, where on the southeast corner stood Emmanuel Episcopal Church. I considered entering the church to look again at the stained glass window given in memory of my grandfather. The window depicted a standing Jesus, palm upraised, with the caption, "I am the light of the world: he that followeth me, walketh not in darkness, but shall have the light of light." I did not understand the connection between this verse and my grandfather who, to the best of my knowledge, only attended church on Christmas and Easter and only then after much cajoling from my grandmother. But I loved the way the light softly filtered through the bold colors of the glass, leaving luminous, yet fragile, reflections on the red velvet of the pew cushions.

Emmanuel Episcopal Church was an inextricable part of my life at the time. On Sundays, I was awarded the responsibility of opening church school by leading the assembled children in Morning Prayer. I rotely mouthed the words, never fully cognizant of their meaning, but nonetheless proud of my ability to glide through the arcane language without stumbling. After Sunday school, I donned my acolyte's vestments and, at precisely 10:45, tugged the bell rope to beckon the small, but devoted congregation. The highlight of any church service at Emmanuel occurred during the singing of the hymns. The church choir was largely comprised of elderly widows cursed with failing voices and blurred eyesight. Consequently, it was not unusual for one or more members of the choir to sing out of sequence the verses of any chosen hymn.

The one time of year the church really outdid itself was the midnight service on Christmas Eve. Wreaths and poinsettias adorned the narthex, nave, and altar, all solely illuminated by candles. In that Emmanuel held the only service at this hour in town, the small church was filled to capacity and many of those present, owing to the late hour and the season, were perceptibly "tipsy," as my grandmother would remark. The Christmas Eve service was a festive one, a night of prayer and music, familiar carols even our choir could not destroy. I recalled the previous year's service when during the recessional, "Joy to the World," my mother's lighted taper momentarily ignited the hair of Susan Markley, Dean's older sister.

I turned left on Church Street and quickly traversed the lot of the Methodist Church, thankful once again that Mother had not deemed it necessary to send me to the Methodists' Vacation Bible School, a torture I had endured for three consecutive summers. I made my way up the delivery alley behind Bailey's Hardware, looking for but not finding discarded soda bottles that could be redeemed for two cents each at the Red & White. I emerged on Main Street, across from the town square with its antebellum courthouse and requisite memorial to Confederate dead. This marble soldier, which commemorated the brave volunteers of Virginia's 54th Regiment, faced south, unwittingly, perhaps, turning its back to the still-advancing enemy.

Nestled under the towering magnolias of the courthouse square was the town library, the destination of that day's journey. The library was a familiar sanctuary for me. My mother insisted that at least two hours a day be devoted to reading. I loved the library. Its dark coolness was comforting and its polished tile floors seemed to echo with the footsteps of many generations of visitors. On this day, as was his custom, Brooks Price sat in a large leather chair in front of the floor to ceiling windows. He was reading the Wall Street Journal, probably the only man in town with the interest or means to do so. Jane Peterson, the librarian, greeted me from behind the desk and, in a polite whisper, inquired as to the health of each member of my family.

"I was wondering when I'd see you again, Will," she said. "I saved a couple of books I thought you might like—*Ivanhoe* by Sir Walter Scott and *The Last of the Mohicans* by Mr. James Fenimore Cooper. They're fine books—full of adventure and even a little romance if you're interested in that sort of thing yet. I'm sure your mother would approve."

My mother had the reputation of being a well-read woman, a Phi Beta Kappa graduate of Hollins College, exiled to our small town when Father came home after the War to help Grandfather run his struggling farm and equipment business. There were few opportunities for intellectual discourse in Bluestone, although Mother, in a fit of despair, did found, and for a number of years sustain, the Ladies' Literary Society.

"Thank you," I answered, "I might look for something else, too, while I'm here. I made my way to the shelves and soon found what I was looking for—*The Mickey Mantle Story*. It was a slim volume, an "as told to" by some beat reporter. While Mantle's background, statistics, and style of play were ingrained in me, I never tired of reading of his exploits, how he was named after Mickey Cochran, the hours as a boy playing catch with his dad—a miner in Oklahoma—his meteoric rise to the big leagues, his phenomenal rookie season. It was all as familiar to me as my own name and I reveled in the definition Mantle's life brought to my own. Besides, this book had a whole middle section full of photographs. Mickey, Yogi Berra, and Roger Maris posed in ineffable ease, bats resting on their shoulders, Louisville Sluggers seemingly as much a part of their bodies as their own muscled arms and legs. Mantle, in the batter's box, bat poised, with number 7 stitched across his pinstriped back. Mantle, torso twisted, arms and lumber extended, eyes watching the flight of the ball toward the right field seats of Yankee Stadium. I knew that during the next few nights, the book would consume the hours before bedtime and fuel my own unrealistic dreams of big league stardom.

I checked out the three books, again thanked Mrs. Peterson, and walked out the door. Seated on a bench at the foot of the steps was a black boy, about my age, reading a book. I thought it odd that he was so nicely dressed, with a crisp white shirt, sharply creased dark trousers and luminously polished black shoes. It was not Sunday or any holiday that I knew of and his appearance seemed so incongruous with the shorts, T-shirts, and tennis shoes favored by myself and my cohorts. Even though he was sitting down I could tell that he was tall and skinny, dodgeball skinny, and his elbows and knees were so pointed that I thought they could, at any minute, puncture the constraints of his clothes. His dark eyes were set deep in his elongated brown face and his hair was close-cropped, almost severe looking. He was, of course, Joe.

Now, admittedly, my experience with black people was limited, despite the fact that they were as much a part of the landscape of my town and county as tobacco and white pines. But most of the blacks I knew, I knew only in relation to some subservient role they assumed in our well-defined society. There was Champ, who loaded sacks of feed and performed other chores at Father's store and who had essentially grown up with my grandfather on my great-grandfather's farm. There was Thelma, Irene, Dorothy May, or whoever the current domestic might be retained by my grandmother. These women never lasted long, dismissed for any number of petty offenses, real or imagined, from forgetting to polish the silver to unapologetically helping themselves to grandmother's "bridge sherry." And, of course, there was Bynum, the elementary school custodian whose eyes were moist and yellow, like fine river silt, and who lived in a makeshift hovel adjacent to the coal bin at the school.

I did not really know, however, any black children although I had certainly seen some being pulled along by frustrated mothers on Saturdays in town. I suppose that is why the sight of Joe intrigued me so. Even more curious to me was the fact that he was reading a book, an exercise I guess I naively felt was reserved for white people. I realized that it had never occurred to me that black people would want to because of what I already intuitively perceived to be limited opportunities. It was a presumptuous attitude on my part, I admit, but one, I maintain, born of innocence. For you see, the doctrine of "separate but equal," thrived in our small town. At the two-doctor clinic on High Street there were separate waiting rooms for "White" and "Colored" patients and, I presumed, separate maladies as well. Mr. Hicks, the proprietor of the movie theater on Main Street relegated his black patrons to the balcony while the town's white citizens sat below. The schools were similarly segregated, a condition preferred by the "darkies," as my grandmother assured me.

Joe did not look up at me and as I paused on the step above him, I realized I would have to be the one to speak. "Hey," I said in a burst of inspiration.

He put his forefinger on the page of the open book so as not to lose his place, turned his head and squinted from the sun peering over my shoulder. "Good morning," he replied in what I would learn was his characteristic quiet tone.

"What are you reading?

"A book about Willie Mays." He stared at me. "The library lady gave it to me."

"Willie Mays? He's pretty good all right. Of course, he's no Mickey Mantle."

There was a pause, a full five seconds, before Joe burst out laughing, his white teeth shattering the uniformity of his dark brown face. I didn't see what was so funny.

"You've got to be kidding," he said. "Mantle can't hold a candle to Willie. If he didn't play for the Yankees, you'd see just how good he'd be."

"What about all those home runs? He hasn't hit all those home runs just because he's a Yankee."

"Having Maris in the line-up doesn't hurt. Who'd you rather pitch to, Mantle or the guy that broke Babe Ruth's record? Look, I know Mantle's a great power hitter, but Mays is a more complete player. He hits for power and for average, plays great defense, and has speed to burn."

There was an urgency in Joe's voice, now. "Mantle can run, too," I said.

"Could run—before he tore his leg up. Have you forgotten what happened in Washington? Besides, are you trying to tell me Mantle could have made that catch off of Vic Wertz in the '54 Series?"

"Yeah, I've seen those pictures. That was a great play."

"I'll say. Only Mays could do that—you know it's true"

"Maybe." I wasn't going to concede the point although I had to admit he could be right, especially when one considered that the current season had been a disappointment to Mantle, owing to lingering injuries. "Well, who won the Series last year?" I countered.

"No thanks to Mantle and his .120 batting average. If Richardson hadn't been standing in exactly the right place, McCovey wins the game and the Series."

This kid knew his stuff. I decided that my best defense would be to change the subject. "My name is Will Rawlings," I offered.

"I know."

"You do? How?"

"You live on Windsor Avenue, right? Well, I live at the college—my dad's a teacher there, a professor. Anyway, the woods behind your house come all the way to the campus."

"I know that. I played in those woods a lot when I was a kid."

"Well, sometimes I sit in those woods and watch you and your friends play baseball. That's how come I know who you are.

The boys in the outfield come in a few steps when 'Will' is up to bat."

"They do not."

"Suit yourself. I'm just telling you how I know your name. My name is Joe—Joe Washington. My father is Dr. Washington."

"Dr. Washington? I thought you said your father was a teacher."

"He is. He's not a doctor doctor; he has a Ph.D. He's an English professor. We just moved here this summer from Bethune-Cookman College in Florida."

Although I wasn't sure what a Ph.D. was, Joe pronounced with such conviction that I figured I was supposed to be impressed. "Do you play baseball?" I asked.

"A lot better than you and your friends, if I do say so myself."

"Well, maybe you could come show us just how good you are someday."

"Maybe. But I've heard the way some of your friends talk. Do you really think Drew Bailey is going to play ball with me? It seems as if his favorite expression is, 'You're as ignorant as a nigger.'"

It was true. Drew resorted to that line of defense during any dispute on the baseball field. While my parents never would have permitted me to say "nigger," many of my contemporaries used the word liberally. I never got used to it. It was an ugly word, a word that I found jarring every time I heard it and especially now, here from Joe. I couldn't defend my friends to Joe, but I wasn't about to denounce them, either.

Look," I said, "I've got to get on home. Maybe I'll see you around sometime."

"Yeah, maybe," said Joe as I turned and walked up the brick sidewalk past the Confederate soldier and across the street. I kept wanting to turn around, to see if Joe was looking at me or if he had returned to his reading, but I kept on in my best rehearsed casual manner.

In those days, pick-up games were the only baseball games in Bluestone and to my knowledge, our afternoon contests represented the longest running series in town. This was pre-Little League days, before adults ruined baseball with uniforms and rules and forever took away the opportunity for boys to settle their own disagreements.

About two o'clock that afternoon, the bicycles started rolling into my driveway, bearing the usual participants of our daily game. Junior and Marvin were there, of course, as were Drew Bailey and Jimmy Hicks, a highly regarded member of these contests because he was the only left-hander among us and could, when all forces were properly aligned, yank an inside pitch down the short right field line and into the woods on the fly for an automatic home run. My mother held Jimmy in less esteem because often in his haste to pull the ball, he would turn on it too quickly and send a foul shot ricocheting off our rambling wooden home or, worse, through an upstairs window. A shattered window meant suspension of play for the day as I pedaled to Bailey's Hardware for a replacement pane and a can of glazing compound.

Dean was there, too, and it was understood that she was to be on my team, no questions asked. Rounding out our group, twelve in all, were a number of younger kids, little brothers or children from the neighborhood, who we tolerated because they filled necessary positions and, in an effort to please us, never tired of retrieving errant balls. There were six us to a team—two outfielders, three infielders, and a pitcher, the catcher provided by the team at bat. I played in the outfield where I could best utilize my imagined speed and my strong arm.

The game that day was much like others of the summer but, as was always the case, different enough to make it unique. My team took an early lead when in the first I doubled home Dean, who herself had doubled after two quick outs. I was stranded at second, however, as little Ray Bailey determinedly, yet futilely, flailed at three of his older brother's offerings. Drew's team went ahead two frames later when he, Marvin, and Junior lined successive singles through the generous gap in our infield created by the absence of Bobby Buford, who had gone home crying when Drew deliberately plucked him on the back with a fastball the previous inning. I remember we tied the game when Jimmy, who fouled two pitches against the house and precariously close to my parents' bedroom window, straightened out Drew's curveball for a solo shot into the woods.

The game remained tied until the last inning when Marvin, a dangerous and unpredictable hitter, came to the plate. In the outfield I shifted a few steps to my left, relying on Marvin's tendency to be a little late in his swing. Marvin took two pitches right down the middle, which having no umpire he was allowed to do, the only strikeouts in our game being swinging ones.

"Come on, Marvin," I yelled. "What are you waiting for." Jimmy came back with another fastball and I started retreating the moment I saw Marvin swing. I think I was in full stride when I actually heard the ball hit the bat, a resounding crack much like the noise Drew made when he did belly flops off the diving board at the town pool. I churned for the woods, but glancing over my left shoulder I think I knew I had little chance of catching the drive. I remember extending my gloved left hand and the frustration of seeing the ball clear the webbing by inches. As Marvin rounded the bases, the ball bounded ahead into the congested pine forest with its thick carpet of needles. When I got to the edge of the woods, I was startled when a figure suddenly emerged from behind one the trees. It was Joe, dressed now in jeans, a T-shirt, and sneakers, holding the ball.

"Willie Mays would have caught it," he said as he tossed the ball underhanded to me.

Joe

I think I spent that first summer at St. George's being pretty much angry at everyone—at my parents who took me away from my friends for reasons I could not fathom, at the people of Bluestone, in my estimation the dullest, most backward town in God's creation, and at myself for being angry when I knew I should be supporting my father and, in general, looking on the bright side of things. But in my mind there was no bright side those first few weeks. It was dutifully reported to me that there were kids my age at the college, but upon investigation, I discovered that all of these kids were girls. I had nothing against girls, you understand; in fact, two of these young ladies in time became good friends to me and remain so to this day. But girls could not, I believed, play ball, ride bikes, and just show me the ropes the way another boy could. Being an only child, I needed a confidant, someone I could express my fears to who would not automatically seek to assure me that everything would be all right.

Late one afternoon, about a week after I first met Will, feeling bored and on the verge of driving my mother crazy from moping around the house, I decided to dig out my tennis racquet from the clutter of my room and go hit some balls. Half of the stuff in my room was still in boxes as I had resisted my mother's pleas to put my belongings away, fearing, I guess, the sense of commitment such a task would demonstrate. It was as if putting my clothes, books, equipment in defined places would be an acknowledgement that I was in this hick town to stay.

Well, anyway, I found my racquet and a can of balls and with a perfunctory, "See ya, Mom," headed over to the tennis court. In that there wasn't anybody to play with, I decided that I would just practice my serve. In Florida, I had been a pretty good player and had successfully competed in some junior tournaments in my home town. I had a strong first serve that was not, however, distinguished by its accuracy. When forced to hit a second serve, which, admittedly, was at least half the time, I lobbed it in—a passive shot that any self-respecting player could anticipate and crush. On this day I decided to experiment with alternative second serves, to come up with something that had some pace to it, but was still accurate.

I took the three balls from the can, stuffed one into the pocket of my shorts and held the other two in my left hand. I tossed the first ball above my head, coiled my knees and sprang my racquet forward like I was chopping wood. The result was not impressive and I tried again, and then again. I gathered the three balls from the base of the net and walked to the other side of the court to repeat the exercise. After about an hour, things started to improve and I really believed I was getting the hang of it. I had made adjustments, and I was consistently getting the serve in, with some speed and a little topspin. It felt good and for the first time all summer I think I was happy. I was in a groove and I could've stayed out them until dark just whacking those white balls. Why not?

Well, I'll tell you why. I was interrupted and actually I heard the sources of this interruption before I saw them. Their shouts startled me in mid-serve and for the first time in a dozen tries, I netted the ball. I could see them up the road, furiously pedaling toward me and taunting each other at the same time. As they got closer, I could tell it was Will and Drew Bailey and they were obviously racing one another. Each clutched a racquet to his handlebars, leaned forward over his bike, and pumped his legs for all he was worth. Drew drove ahead as they neared the court and as he veered onto the gravel path that led to the playing surface, he had opened up a sizable lead. He slammed on his brakes, spinning his bike around and spewing gravel against the chain-link fence that surrounded the lined concrete. He sat erect on his seat, facing the road now, smiling, as Will, defeated, rolled in beside him.

"You stupid son of a bitch. I told you you couldn't beat me. You buy the sodas after the match. Unless, of course, you want to make it double or nothing."

It was at this point that Will saw me and as he stared at the court, Drew turned around and eyed me for the first time. "Hey," Will said.

"Hey, yourself." I walked to the net and retrieved the ball I had just hit. I strolled deliberately back to the service line, bounced the ball twice, and smoked a serve past my imaginary opponent. Ace. I didn't look at the two interlopers, just calmly walked to the other end of the court, gathered the three balls and continued my routine. Ace. Ace. Ace. I was loving it. Drew and Will had dismounted from their bikes and were sitting now on the bench outside the midcourt gate. I could hear what they were saying and as I went about my practice, more deliberate now than before, it was apparent that Drew was getting annoyed.

"How long is he planning on staying out there?"

"Shhh," whispered Will. "He'll hear you."

"So? I'm not sitting around all day while some colored boy pretends he's Rod Laver."

"He lives here. I guess he's got more right to play here than we do."

"How come you know so much about him?"

"I just do. Anyway, be quiet, for God's sake."

"Well, he'd better hurry up, that's all I got to say."

I just kept pounding in those serves, not faulting once while they were there. I figured I had disrupted their routine—they weren't used to finding someone on the court in the summer time and it was clear that they were not pleased, especially Drew. I didn't know how often they played, but from having spied on their baseball games I knew what kind of players they'd be. Will would favor the baseline, try to keep the ball in play. He was probably the kind of guy who would run around every backhand and be content to let you beat yourself. Drew, on the other hand, would be all power and intimidation. Serve, rush the net. Hit everything with as much ferocity as possible. A racquet slammer—you could count on it. I remember thinking that I'd love the opportunity to play him, to frustrate him. Ace. Ace. Ace.

I figured I had probably made my point—whatever it might have been—and was about to relinquish the court when Drew shouted, "Hey, boy! How about letting somebody else play awhile?" I turned to look at them, but Will's eyes did not meet mine. He was staring at the ground, nervously spinning his racquet between his legs. Drew returned my gaze, his eyes informing me that this was not unchartered territory for him. I considered my options. I sure didn't want a confrontation because, quite honestly, I knew that Drew could beat the crap out of me if he had a mind to. But at twelve years old, saving face is important and no one, I knew, could put a price on self-respect.

I was just about to say something that would have gotten me in a lot of trouble, when we were all distracted by a car that slowed and then pulled to a stop parallel to the court. It was my father, who leaned his head out the window and shouted to me, "Joe, your mama says come on home now for dinner. I have to run get some milk, but be right there." He waited for me to move. Perhaps he just wanted to make sure I had heard him or, perhaps, he sensed something was wrong. I'm not sure. But he sat in the idling car while I gathered the tennis balls and walked off the court.

"See ya," Will said as I hurried by.

"Yea, see ya," Drew repeated. I reached the road, looked up at my dad and without a word, turned toward home. He drove off in the opposite direction, confused, I'm sure, by my reticence.

I was confused, too. It was clear my father's fortuitous arrival had saved me from a potentially disastrous situation. But it was also clear that matters were left unresolved; I couldn't figure out how I felt about that. Was it important that I save my self-esteem by answering Drew's supposed challenge? Was it necessary for me to somehow win Will's approbation? I didn't know. And while I was grateful on the one hand for my father's intercession, I was also angry. It was just like him to come to my rescue, and it was embarrassing in a way. And I was embarrassed, as only a twelve-year-old can be, by the actions of a parent. Maybe I didn't need his help. No, I definitely didn't need his help.

The table was set when I arrived home. As usual, Mother's fine china and crystal were on display, and her silver, too. She insisted on it and I am reminded today as I watch my own children running hither and yon, gulping down processed junk, that our typical family meal was anything but. Our meals were elaborate, almost formal occasions and three times a day, when I wasn't in school, we sat down as a family. There was always ample food at dinner, something I knew I took for granted. There was fried chicken or roast pork, mashed potatoes, and green beans simmered down to sweet resignation. My father believed it was important that we shared these times and he expected each of us to give a full accounting of his day and his thoughts and he obligingly set the example by relating the minutiae of his daily existence.

I washed my hands, by which time Daddy had returned with the milk. He poured it into a silver pitcher and brought it to the table where Mother and I waited. He held the chair for Mother, my cue that I could now sit down, and he sat down himself. We held hands as he intoned the blessing. "Heavenly Father, thank you for this provender we are about to receive, and for thy bountiful goodness and mercy. Bless this food to our use and us to thy service. In Christ's name we pray. Amen."

"Amen," we repeated.

As he began serving us copious quantities of Mother's home cooking, he initiated a litany of his day's activities. "I trust everyone had a fruitful day," he began but did not pause to acknowledge any response from us. "I had an intriguing experience which you might find of some interest. Don't chew with your mouth open, son. A young lady—a Miss Boykin— came to my office and announced that she would like to take my Advanced Composition class in the fall. She is a rising senior and I asked her what other English classes she had taken. 'None,' she replied. She is a Home Economics major and I honestly feel she had come to college with the idea of using her domestic skills to attract a suitable husband. I pulled her record after she left—she's a scholarship student from down around Smoky Ordinary—the first in her family to go to college. More beans, Lucille? I have a feeling that her plan to snare a husband has thus far failed her— the poor thing is pretty homely looking—and she's determined, perhaps, to explore whatever else the world may have to offer."

"Now, Herbert, I hope you haven't judged her too harshly. You have to admire someone who is interested in improving herself."

"Precisely, dear."

It occurs to me now that Daddy's narrative struck a familiar chord with my mother. She herself had come from humble beginnings. My parents had met in college and afterwards, my mother, who I believe has more natural sense than any human being I have ever encountered, quit a fledgling career as a biology teacher, which she had pursued for three years while Daddy was in graduate school, to ornament my father's ambitions and to devote herself to my upbringing.

"Anyway, I told Miss Boykin that I would have to see a writing sample before I could admit her to the class and if she was amenable to the idea, I could give her a topic to write about on the spot. I thought the suggestion would discourage her, but it didn't. She said she was ready, so I cleared some books off the table in the corner and gave her some paper and a pen. I told her she had thirty minutes to write a 2-3 page composition about a vivid memory or experience from her childhood. I returned to my desk where I pretended to busy myself, but really I spent the time watching Miss Boykin. I have never in my life seen someone so actively engaged in the process of writing. Her whole body seemed involved in her task. Her arms and legs kept rhythm with her hand as her pen raced across the page. It was as if she were getting inspiration from the soles of her feet and the energy was coursing through her toes and up to every part in her body. She was so animated, it was truly amazing to watch. She didn't stop pushing that pen the whole time, either. I coughed a couple of times to see if I might distract her, but I believe she didn't even hear me."

"Oh, Herbert, you're exaggerating."

"Lucille, I swear I'm not. The girl was possessed. It was like I was back at Mt. Zion Baptist Church with my great Aunt Callie, watching somebody receive the spirit." He laughed at the memory and took another forkful of mashed potatoes.

"When I called 'time' on her, she put down the pen and sheepishly handed me five pages of looping script. I quickly shuffled through the paper and the first thing I noticed was that it was all one paragraph. This made me skeptical, of course, and I prepared myself for some pedestrian treatise on 'My Favorite Christmas' or 'The Day my Dog Died,' but as I started to read the composition, I was immediately entranced. It was a story about how, as a girl, she had such vivid dreams and how she decided one day to collect them. She began writing the dreams down and putting them in an empty jar—one of those big jars like you see in country stores full of pig knuckles—and soon she was collecting other people's dreams, too. She asked the members of her family to tell her their dreams. And her friends, as well. She wrote each of them down and put them in the jar. She kept this up for over a year and amassed about 150 dreams. Isn't that amazing? And she still has the jar and from time to time reaches into it, pulls out a slip of paper, and is transported to another time and place."

"What a wonderful story," Mother said. "It just goes to show, you can't judge a book by its cover."

"True enough. Of course, the grammar was atrocious and her vocabulary seems very limited, but it was an enchanting composition nonetheless."

"So, are you going to let her in the class?" I asked innocently.

"Yes indeed, son. One is always thankful to come across something that is fresh. I brought the paper home with me. Perhaps you would like to read it after dinner?"

"Yes sir," I replied to this request that was not a request.

Daddy continued. "I guess it's truly a miracle that any of the children at this college can read or write. Most of them have grown up in the most abominable circumstances and attended school only when the school board had money left over after meeting the needs of the white children. Sometimes I despair of being able to teach them anything."

"They may be uneducated, Herbert, but they are not ignorant," said Mother. "Look at Miss Boykin. Now she sounds like someone of tremendous potential. And just think of yourself, dear, and how far you've come. Where would you be if your teachers had given up on you?"

"Right you are, dear." He added, tenderly, "As always."

Daddy turned his attention to me. "More mashed potatoes, son? No? Well, tell us about your day. Who were those two boys at the tennis court?"

"Their names are Will Rawlings and Drew Bailey."

"How do you know them?"

"I don't really. I kind of met Will at the library. He likes baseball."

"Was everything okay with you and those boys? I mean, I got the impression that there was a problem."

I knew he hated asking this question. You could tell it made him uncomfortable. He liked to believe, deep down, that times had changed, that the world was a vastly different place than when he was a boy. But he was enough of a realist to understand that the world was much the same now as then. Mother's fork was poised above her plate, halted by the tone of Daddy's question. She looked at me expectantly. They worried about me too much. It was times like this that made me wish for brothers and sisters, someone else to share the burden of parental anxiety.

I tried to allay their fears. "No, there wasn't really a problem. They were just surprised I was on the court when they wanted to play, that's all. It was no big deal. Drew acted like he wanted to start something, but he was just huffing and puffing."

"Herbert, do you know these boys?" Mother asked. She wanted the matter more defined, devoid of subtlety. Who were these boys and where did they come from and just how much should she be worried?

"Well, I know the families," he answered. "Drew Bailey's father owns the hardware store. He seems nice enough—a little brusque, perhaps. I do know that he won't extend credit to any colored person, whereas he will to his white customers. That's about all I know of him. And Lucille, you know I'm familiar with the Rawlings. I know them well, as a matter of fact. My grandfather and John Rawlings grandfather grew up together on the same farm, out by the river on the old Rawlings' place, the remnant of Seven Oaks, the family plantation. I assume, although I don't know it for sure, that my grandfather's people had been slaves there. In fact, I wouldn't be surprised if my grandfather had a little Rawlings blood in him, if you know what I mean."

I did, but I could not fathom it really. It was hard enough to accept that my ancestors might have been slaves to Will's ancestors. It was all too much to consider that one of these ancestors might have been the same for both of us. I wondered how much of this Will knew.

"Herbert, you don't know any of this to be fact," said my mother, who, of course, had heard these stories before, but who was anxious to protect me from "ancient history." She had been reluctant to come to Bluestone but did so because she understood my father's need to validate his own beginnings.

"No, I don't, but it's what I've always been told. By my father, and my grandfather before him. Besides, how else would you explain the fact that after the plantation broke up, the family gave my grandfather 40 acres for himself? By all accounts, the Rawlings clan was not a naturally munificent one. Anyway, my father grew up on those 40 acres and, consequently, had contact with Billy Rawlings, John's father. But I think both my father and Billy Rawlings knew they weren't cut out to be farmers. Billy Rawlings moved to town and began his farmer's supply business while my father, like a number of other colored folks, went to

Detroit and got a steady job on the assembly line. This was right after World War I when the automobile industry was taking off. Now you know my father never shied away from hard work, and, in time, he achieved about as much responsibility as a Negro could in those days. So when the Depression hit, he was able to hold on to his job. Eventually, he even managed to forge what you might call a middle-class existence for himself and his family. He owned his own car, which was pretty rare, and a home, which was more unusual still. Yet, he never forgot where he came from and he didn't want me to forget, either. When I was 14, just a little older than you, Joe, he put me on a bus and sent me down here to spend the summer on Granddaddy's farm. My mother was hysterical about the whole prospect, I remember. She was from Detroit and I believe she felt I would be lynched for sure in Virginia. But my father was insistent. He said it was important for me to learn the value of hard work and to understand what it was like to have earth under your fingernails. Besides, he felt it was important that I spend some time with my grandfather, more time than the few days every other Christmas when the whole family drove down for a hurried visit.

"I'll never forget that bus ride. I was nervous—scared would be more like it. I really didn't know my grandfather well. He was a quiet man, but one who smiled at whatever the world handed him. He knew that life was not fair, but you did what you could and sometimes things might work out. I remember sitting in the back of that bus, clutching to my lap a sack full of sandwiches my mother had made and watching the land roll by, the red clay fields of tobacco and the broad hunched backs of the black people who worked them.

"But it was a wonderful summer. My grandfather accepted me immediately and taught me all those things he felt I should know—how to fish, how to predict the weather by looking at the sky, even how to birth a calf. I'll never forget it."

"Please, Herbert, you're boring the boy to death," Mother said with a sense of urgency in her voice. But in truth, I wasn't bored. Normally, I had little tolerance for Daddy's stories, but I was fascinated by this personal glimpse into his past. I wondered why I had never heard this tale before and why, more importantly, I was hearing it now. Was it somehow connected to the episode at the tennis court? Did the mere mention of Will Rawlings suggest to my father that he unburden himself?

"That was when I met John Rawlings," Daddy continued. "One evening I went with Granddaddy up to the Rawlings's place to sharpen some hand tools on their grinding wheel in the barn. John was there, a couple of years older than me, putting out some hay for his horse. Granddaddy introduced us, but John didn't have much to say. I know I sure didn't. I remember he called granddaddy by his first name, Joe—your namesake, son. Called him 'Old Joe,' as a matter of fact. I was embarrassed for Granddaddy, that some boy could call him 'Old Joe.' I had never heard that term of address before. He was always "Mr. Washington" to the colored folk. The familiarity offended me. Anyway, I ran into John Rawlings a couple of more times that summer, but he never paid me no mind, no more than he would a dog sleeping in the shade."

The tone of this last comment was uncharacteristically bitter. I remember thinking that there was more to this story than Daddy was telling, even now in this unusually revelatory moment. He paused, took a couple of peremptory bites of green beans, and then put his fork back down.

"Well, sorry for the digression," he said. "I was telling you about my father. Now the one thing he wanted more than anything else was for his children to go to college. He worked and he saved so that this dream might become a reality."

He was on familiar ground, now, and the words rolled easily off his tongue. Besides, I knew the story by heart, I had heard it so many times. How my grandfather would review his children's homework every night, how he spanked them if they brought home any grade below an 'A,' how proud he had been of my father when he graduated from college and three years later, received his doctorate. Grandfather had died a year after that, six months before my own birth, but apparently he had spent the last months of his life telling everyone, even strangers, that his son was a "Doctor." At the time, I'm not sure I appreciated the story of my grandfather's life, but I was conscious that there were high expectations for me and that any effort less than my best was not acceptable. Finally, Daddy paused and stared somewhere beyond my head at a distant point on the floral wallpaper.

"Well, maybe it's time I renewed my acquaintance with John Rawlings," Daddy said. He pushed his chair back from the table, his signal that he was through with his meal. Mother rose abruptly and began clearing the dishes. I got up to help but she insisted, rather forcefully I thought, that she didn't need any help, thank you. When she was in the kitchen, out of earshot, Daddy leaned over and whispered confidentially, "Your mother thinks I should let bygones be bygones." We could hear her rattling dishes in the sink. "She wasn't overly enthusiastic about moving here—too much 'history' she said—but once I made the decision, she supported it. Your mother's a rare woman, son. Don't ever forget it. I try not to."

Mother opened the door from the kitchen, as if on cue. "Could I interest anyone in some pie?"

"I believe you could find a couple of takers in here," answered Daddy, winking conspiratorially. "What do you say, Joe?"

"Sounds good to me."

Mother retreated to the kitchen and reappeared moments later with two plates containing thick wedges of pecan pie, my favorite. She set the plates in front of us and sat down again.

"You're not having any, Lucille?"

"No, I don't believe so. I'm not that hungry this evening."

"Well, it's delicious as usual," said Daddy savoring his first forkful. "I just don't know how you get the crust so flaky."

"It's store bought."

"Isn't that amazing," Daddy weakly concluded.

There was an uncomfortable silence where all that could be heard was the clinking of our forks against the plates. I was aware that Mother's eyes were fixed on me, staring at me. I concentrated on the pie, my own eyes lowered.

"I had an interesting experience this morning," Mother suddenly said.

"Do tell," Daddy said, relieved, as was I, that her voice had broken through the miasma of the room.

"I was in the checkout line at the Red & White, waiting to pay for the groceries—except the milk, of course, which I somehow forgot—and there was an old colored woman in the line in front of me. She was a pitiful old thing, bundled up in an overcoat, never mind that it was at least ninety-five degrees today, and her hair was up in a kerchief. She was frail with a dowager's hump and she had her groceries in one of those pull-along carts so I figured she must have walked to the store. Her groceries consisted mostly of bread, a few tins of potted meat, and some cat food. The checkout boy, some white child not old enough to shave, rang up her items and announced the total as $7.65. The old woman reached into the pocket of her coat and pulled out a little change purse, which she unsnapped. It was taking her some time, as you can imagine, and the lady behind me kept sighing and harumphing like she was being terribly inconvenienced so that I finally had to turn around and stare at her. I think she got the message."

I was sure she had. Believe me, I knew that stare and there was no ambiguity as to its meaning.

"Anyway, the old lady reached in to the change purse and

pulled out six rumpled dollar bills. She handed them to the checkout boy who seemed annoyed that he had to straighten them out and then she dumped the rest of the contents of the purse on the counter. There were mostly pennies and nickels with a few dimes and quarters scattered about. A few buttons, too. The boy counted it all and told she only had a $1.58 in change. The old woman didn't say anything. The checkout boy spoke again. 'Look, you've got a $1.58 in change and six one dollar bills. That makes $7.58 total. "You're seven cents short." You could tell he was proud of himself for being so good in numbers. He probably flunked math last year in high school."

Daddy laughed at this comment, one of his snort-through-the-nose laughs.

"It wasn't funny, Herbert; it was pitiful. Anyway, the old lady said in a voice as dry as parchment, 'I ain't got no mo' money' and the boy, not missing a beat said, 'Well, aunty, you'll have to put something back, Aunty. I mean, can you believe it Herbert? Honestly, you'd never know it's 1963. Well, that's when I stepped in. 'I'll pay the seven cents,' I said, putting a nickel and two pennies on the counter. 'Why don't you go ahead and bag the lady's groceries.' She looked at me and said, 'Thank you, missy.' Now, no one's called me 'missy' in twenty years I reckon. That sweet old thing. I murmured something back to her and the checkout boy put her bag in the cart. She smiled a toothless smile at me and walked towards the door as I started putting my own groceries up on the counter.

"As you might imagine, the checkout boy and I didn't exchange any pleasantries as he rang up my groceries. When he announced my total, I doled out the money to him, but I deliberately shorted him one cent. I knew he wouldn't say anything and he didn't. I guess I wanted the satisfaction of having him make up the difference at the end of the day. I know it was wrong, but we take our victories when we can."

I couldn't believe my mother had purposely cheated someone. But, as I was beginning to realize, it is best not to be governed by preconceptions. That summer was a time of revelations, both good and bad, and this insight into my mother was just another in what was to become a series of distorted illusions.

"I got the groceries in the car and was just heading home when I saw that old woman trudging along the sidewalk, yanking her cart behind her. I pulled over, got out of the car and asked her if I could give her a ride home. She said she would appreciate it if it wouldn't 'misaccomodate' me. I put her cart in the back seat and helped her up front. She said she lived in Mayfield, you know, that little Negro settlement just outside the town limits. She told me her name was Dallas and during the whole ride, she kept asking me who my 'people' were. I had a hard time getting her to understand I wasn't from this area. She said she had heard of your folks, Herbert, but that she was a 'town darkey,' as she put it, and had never really known too many people from out in the county. She takes in ironing for white people, fifty cents a load, and as far as I could figure, that's her only income.

"Herbert, you wouldn't have believed that house. Just a four-room clapboard box with chinks so big she must freeze in the winter. Of course her bathroom was a privy out back and the kitchen had some prehistoric icebox and a woodstove. The ironing board was set up in the middle of the kitchen and the iron was plugged into an overhead outlet with one naked light bulb.

I helped her bring her groceries in—I had to shoo away a half dozen cats from the table so I could set the bag down—and she wouldn't let me leave until she showed me a picture of her 'chillun.' It was a Christmas post card, you know the kind with the photograph and the pre-printed message. 'Seasons Greetings' it said with 'Lawrence, Carolyn, Larry, Betty, and Judith' stamped across the bottom. There was no handwritten message at all. No 'Hope you are well,' no 'We love you,' no nothing. She got the same card the paper boy did, I reckon. They live in Newark and Lawrence, that's her boy, has some sort of government job. She told me the last time she had seen them was the summer before Judith was born and Judith was four, if she was a day.

"Herbert, I couldn't get out of that house fast enough. I know it sounds terrible, but I believed if I had stayed any longer, I would've started crying. I told her I'd come see her sometime, but I'm not sure I could go back."

We were all quiet and I wondered if Mother might in fact start crying now. I hoped not. The times I had felt the absolute worse in my young life were the rare times I witnessed my mother moved to tears. My attitude was a selfish one, but one I did not know how to mitigate. I could tell my father was searching for the right thing to say and I think it was then I first understood the limits of love and the frustration of not knowing how to comfort the person in your life for whom you would give your life if need be. Daddy stared at the dessert plate in front of him, sticky with the remnants of pecan pie.

"Joe," he said, "help me clear the rest of these dishes."

I almost jumped out of my chair, eager to escape my own futility, and carried my plate and empty milk glass through the swinging door into the kitchen. There, Daddy put his arm around me, a gesture so rare that it momentarily startled me.

"Son, how about if tomorrow you and I go meet Dallas, maybe take her a few things? What do you say?"

I just nodded.

Will

My grandmother was a professional Southerner. She took her job seriously and was unstinting in the defense of her homeland. She never compromised her beliefs, refusing, for example, to ever ride in her friend Sue Bolling's Lincoln Continental. After all, my grandmother reasoned, she could never accept as a means of transportation any vehicle named after the Great Emancipator. Her afternoon toddy was made with Rebel Yell, the only bourbon sold exclusively below the Mason-Dixon line. As a child, any transgression I might commit invoked from my grandmother a reproachful, "What would General Lee think?" Over her living room mantle she even had a caricature of an unrepentant Confederate soldier uttering the oath, "Forget Hell."

The Civil War, or the Late Unpleasantness as my grandmother referred to the conflict, was a source of unbridled interest and mystery for her. Growing up only two houses away, I had limitless access to my grandmother and her stories of Lee, Jackson, and my own favorite, Colonel John S. Mosby, Grey Ghost of the Confederacy. Under Grandmother's tutelage, I managed to develop a passionate distrust of Yankees and a whimsical notion that one day the South would rally and redress the wrongs committed against her a mere hundred years ago.

And in her own way, my grandmother did her best to perpetuate the Old South and its "peculiar institution" of slavery. I have already described how she imperiously lorded over a series of maids whose misfortune it was to be in her service. And Champ, the handyman at Father's store was constantly victimized by Grandmother's whims. Often he was hastily summoned to cut her grass or perhaps move some piece of furniture before the arrival of the ladies of the bridge club.

So when the rumors started circulating a couple of weeks before school was to open, it was easy to predict which side of the issue my grandmother would endorse. According to Bob Hart, the well-meaning but ineffectual principal of Robert E. Lee Elementary, four Negro children had registered to attend our previously all-white school. He would not divulge the names of the children, but offered his opinion that "outside agitators," in the form of the Richmond headquarters of the NAACP, were somehow to blame. These revelations, as can be imagined, caused much consternation in the white populous of Bluestone and many earnest discussions, official and unofficial, ensued. Almost overnight a segregationist academy was created and fundraising efforts on its behalf begun. Four trailers were leased and placed on a fallow field at Earl Temple's farm, two miles outside of town. Parents began enrolling their children at Bluestone Academy, "Home of the Bulldogs," and among the first to sign-up were my baseball friends, Jimmy Hicks and Marvin Freeman. Teachers were recruited to the Academy with good faith promises, although, to their credit, Miss Julia Lee, Miss Elfie, and other stalwarts of Robert E. Lee Elementary refused to leave, believing that education should be color blind.

I remember many whispered conversations between my parents during those two weeks. They were, of course, discussing where I should attend my last year of elementary school; yet never once did either parent consult with me concerning this issue.

My brother and sister were unaffected by these perturbations because, according to "informed sources," no colored children had registered to attend the high school.

Of course my grandmother insisted that I attend the Academy, even offering, I later learned, to pay my tuition. She was adamant in her assertion that no grandchild of hers should share a facility with the children of "common field hands." I remember that I received my grandmother's proclamation with a certain degree of effrontery.

I'm not trying to make myself noble or anything; after all, I probably subscribed to the widely held conviction that black people were inherently inferior to white, but I was made uncomfortable by grandmother's zealousness on the issue. I guess you could say that I had an uneasy relationship with my grandmother at the time. I loved her devotedly, but I found it uncomfortable to be around her when she allowed her prejudices to surface. I don't think she was maliciously bigoted, but her use of words such as "darkies" struck me as archaic and inappropriate. I guess I should have been more forgiving of her and cognizant of her background and her circumstances, but I wanted her to be perfect. It was not enough that she loved me and was forgiving of my faults; I wanted her to assume this attitude towards others and not seek to explain their shortcomings, real or imagined, as a matter of race or religion.

Ultimately my parents overruled my grandmother, declaring that I should continue my education at Robert E. Lee Elementary. I'm not sure what led them to that decision. It could be that my mother's egalitarian sensibilities won out or, perhaps, it was because my father, a merchant, feared some potential economic repercussions from his black customers. Also, my father, as senior warden at Emmanuel Episcopal was automatically on the board at St. George's College. Maybe he realized that the colored children picked to integrate our school would likely come from that community and he was cognizant of the hypocrisy involved in sending his own child to an exclusionary institution. Whatever the reason, it was a courageous decision in that my father had spent a lifetime deferring to the wishes of his mother. I'm sure that he failed to persuade Grandmother that the decision was a judicious one, but perhaps he used his connection to the college to mollify her anger. It could be he appeased her by appealing to some latent missionary zeal within her. For the Episcopal Church was the one thing my grandmother valued as much as the South.

Grandmother was a stalwart member of Emmanuel Episcopal Church. She was the head of the altar guild for as long as anyone could remember and even assisted the vestry on the infrequent occasions when a search for a new minister was required. For the men of the vestry, in their collective wisdom, understood that any cleric they hired without Grandmother's personal stamp of approval was doomed to failure. Of course, Grandmother unfailingly attended every service at Emmanuel, arriving with startling precision three minutes after the first chords of the processional hymn. And woe be to the unsuspecting visitor or newcomer who innocently sat himself in her accustomed pew, the one adjacent to my grandfather's stained glass window. Grandmother's Christian charity extended only so far, and she would unequivocally announce to the visitor that he would need to find another seat.

I remember one briefly-tenured minister who audaciously wanted us to "pass the peace" during the service—to turn on cue and greet our neighbors. Grandmother would have nothing to do with this "custom." She refused to acknowledge the salutations of those around her and offered none herself. For Grandmother, a church service was not a time for conviviality and, after three frustrating weeks, the practice was suspended.

Services at Emmanuel were unfailingly predictable and most

of the communicants, I'm sure, preferred it that way. Except for special Sundays in the church year, the service consisted of two lessons, three hymns, one sonorous sermon, and the offertory. We all knew the ritual—the Apostles' Creed, the Nicene Creed, the Lord's Prayer—and we sped through the recitations without the assistance of the Book of Common Prayer. Even Communion, the first Sunday of every month, had a feeling of reckless abandon to it and it was rare that my father, Jim Bailey, Hank Newsom, president of the bank, and Henry Lafoon, Clerk of the Court, could not honor their noon tee-off time at Bluestone Country Club. These services were characterized by their constancy, the off-key antics of the choir, the solemn sermons of Dr. Taylor, our elderly minister. The sound of Jim Bailey in the front pew rattling the change in his pocket was annoying, yet reassuring and on hot summer days the ladies of the congregation valiantly tried to stir up a breeze by swishing the New Testament scene cardboard hand fans donated by Williams' Funeral Home ("Eternity Made Affordable"). After the recessional, brief pleasantries were exchanged and my mother, brother, sister, and myself adjourned to Grandmother's house for a glass of sherry and as many of the colored sugar wafers as we cared to eat.

It was the Sunday of Labor Day weekend that the ritual changed forever. Mother and Father had gone to Richmond for the weekend for a convention of the Retail Merchants Association and the opportunity it afforded Father to compare notes with other grain dealers and farm equipment salesmen from around the state. These contacts produced contradictory effects in Father. I believe they depressed him because, after a college education and seeing the world in the War, he longed to be more than a small town merchant in an inherited business. Yet he was sometimes buoyed by these conversations with his colleagues, conversations that led revealed his astute business acumen and assured him he was faring better than most of his contemporaries. Mother managed to strike a balance between attending scheduled events for the wives and launching out on her own for shopping forays to Thalheimer's, Miller & Rhodes, and La Vogue. My brother and sister were also gone this weekend, staying with the families of different friends in rented cottages at Sandbridge, strutting on its wide beach, each hoping to meet the love of their dreams, but not each other.

I was spending the weekend with Grandmother, sleeping in Father's childhood room with its artifacts that seemed so disassociated from the man I knew. There was a photograph of him and his two sisters as children. Father's hair was cut in a page-boy and he, clad in his blue sailor suit, stared haughtily at the camera. There was a photo of him and Tommy Palmer, brown and impossibly skinny teenagers flanking a marlin they had battled for the better part of a day on a fishing trip to Florida with Mr. Palmer. There was a college-age picture, too. Father, hair slicked back and neck stretching from the confines of his starched shirt and rep tie, chin tilting upward as if to precariously balance some unseen object, smoke curling from the cigarette poised in his hand. As I stared at these pictures from the old four-poster bed, I was aware of the independent spirit displayed in each. Here was a boy, a man who knew where he was going, who would not be tied down by the mundane offerings of his world, The attitude seemed to contrast so with the sober, reliable, devoted family man I knew my father to be. I, of course, was glad he was such a man, but as a dreamer myself, I wondered at the manner in which events conspire to alter one's visions of the future.

On Saturday night, Grandmother had taken me to eat at the dining room of the motel out by the four-lane. Other than the poolroom lunch counter, the motel was the only establishment in town that offered a place to dine. The food was not particularly good and on this night I had an unimpressive dinner of fried fish, succotash, kale, and two pieces of coconut chess pie. Back home after dinner, we talked awhile, revisiting Jackson's Valley Campaign and the brave heroics of the VMI Keydets at the Battle of New Market. I went to bed early, briefly struggling with the hyperbolic exploits of Natty Bumpo and his trusted rifle, Deerslayer.

The next morning, Grandmother fixed breakfast, a rare exercise for one who so abjured cooking in any manner. We had scrambled eggs, fried ham, biscuits, and coffee with a harsh chicory taste that I softened with milk. My parents didn't allow me to drink coffee, which was fine with me because I didn't particularly care for it anyway. But when Grandmother offered it, I couldn't refuse because, in some ways, I considered us to be equals and friends, and as long as our discussions didn't stray beyond the Civil War or family genealogy, we were.

After breakfast, we went to dress for church, a task that took me considerably less time than it did Grandmother. I was glad to he accompanying her to church, having abdicated my acolyte duties for the day to Dave Settle. I sat on the front porch for thirty minutes, getting up repeatedly to glance in the hall at the grandfather clock and its incremental march toward 11:00. Finally, at five of, Grandmother emerged and I had to admit that her time had been well-spent. She looked regal with her floral dress, pearls, gloves, and matching shoes and hat. I held the driver's side door of the Cadillac open for her and scurried around to the passenger seat for the two-block drive to Emmanuel. As Grandmother parked the car, I could hear the strains of the processional hymn through the open doors of the church. We walked toward these doors, Grandmother casually, I more anxiously. I wanted to get into Church as quickly as possible because, as a twelve-year-old, I was self-conscious about making an entrance and, unlike my grandmother, I did not like to draw attention to myself in any way. By the time we crossed the threshold, however, the hymn had concluded. Dr. Taylor paused before beginning the first lesson while Grandmother and I walked to the vacant pew.

It was during the second lesson that the ritual changed. I guess it was the pronounced hesitancy in Dr. Taylor's voice that alerted us, for when we followed his eyes to the back of the church, there, sitting alone in the last pew, was Dr. Washington. I recognized him from the tennis court, and as our collective gaze enveloped him, an eerie quiet engulfed the room. Alarmed by the sudden silence, June Nelson led the other four members of the choir, whose view was obstructed by the organ, to investigate the cause of this aberrant hush. When they saw the solitary black man, they scuttled back to their station. Jim Bailey stopped rattling his change and looked across the aisle to fellow vestryman, Henry Lafoon. No one knew what to do, including, I suspect, Dr. Washington. Dr. Taylor tried to continue his reading, but faltered, aware that the real lesson was in the church and not on the page in front of him. The poor man was helpless. He did not know where his allegiance to God ended and his allegiance to his communicants began.

After much elbow jabbing from their wives, Henry and Jim walked to the back of the church. Dr. Washington never flinched, but allowed the two men to clasp him by the elbows and usher him towards the door. The whole scene unfolded in slow motion like the moments leading to a car crash when time is retarded and you are acutely aware of every detail. Dr. Washington did not protest—he was too well-mannered for that—but as this trinity reached the door, my grandmother suddenly called out. "Henry! Jim!" she shouted. "Just a minute, please." We stared at her, all of us, and although it seems a cliche to say I could hear the blood pounding in my temples, it was nonetheless true. "Dr. Washington is here as my guest," she continued. "I'm sure he didn't see me when he first came in. Please allow him to join me."

I beamed. Of course I knew my grandmother was lying; she had not invited Dr. Washington to church. In fact, I was surprised she even knew who Dr. Washington was. I didn't care. Jim and Henry were not about to argue with my grandmother. She had practically raised them and no self-professed gentleman would protest against a woman who has changed his diapers. They released their grip on Dr. Washington and he walked to our pew, slipped in beside me, and gravely nodded to my grandmother. With lowered heads Jim and Henry returned to their seats and Dr. Taylor continued the lesson about Paul's conversion on the road to Damascus.

I remember the rest of the service as a flood of sensations. I was impressed with the soft texture of Dr. Washington's dark flannel suit and the way it contrasted with the crisp starchiness of his white shirt. I still recall the tangled sweetness of his smell, the strong aroma of his aftershave competing with the pungent clinical odor of his processed hair. His beautiful baritone voice took us all by surprise. During the sermon hymn, which Dr. Taylor announced as #263, not #174 as posted, Dr. Washington sang with fervor and, to me, music was suddenly a thing of beauty, not a cacophonous ordeal. As I held the hymnal high between my grandmother and Dr. Washington, the words took on new meaning:

In Christ there is no East or West,
In him no South or North,
But one great fellowship of love
Throughout the whole wide earth.

In him shall true hearts ev'rywhere
Their high communion find

His service is a golden cord
Close binding all mankind.

Join hands, then, brothers of the faith,
Whate'er your race may be!
Who serves my Father as a son
Is surely kin to me.

In Christ now meet both East and West,
In him meet South and North,
All Christly souls are one in him,
Throughout the whole wide earth.

I wanted to believe those words and it seemed to me at that moment that there was no reason why I shouldn't.

Dr. Taylor's sermon was inspired. He abandoned his weekly Old Testament history lesson to speak extemporaneously of God's benevolence. He reminded us that we were all His children and were all equal in His eyes. I sincerely think that this was the shining moment of Dr. Taylor's career. A man of refinement and good conscience, he had been exiled by the Church hierarchy to serve our small parish until he could retire.

It was after the sermon that I witnessed Dr. Taylor's euphoria melt away. During communion, my grandmother, myself, and Dr. Washington were the only ones who went to the altar rail to receive the bread and wine. We returned to our seats and Dr. Taylor raised the chalice to beckon the rest of the congregation. No one moved. Puzzled, I turned around in my seat, looking at those behind me. At first I didn't understand and I felt an urgent need to remind them of their responsibilities. Why was no one responding? I looked to my grandmother, but like Dr.

Washington, she stared resolutely forward. Dr. Taylor lifted the chalice again, more feebly this time; the congregation remained immobile. It dawned on me. They would not partake of Christ's blood after the cup had touched Dr. Washington's lips.

I slumped in the pew as Dr. Taylor finished the service. My faith in my fellow man was at an all time low. The recessional hymn was my favorite and I sang with as much conviction as I could muster.

I sing a song of the saints of God,
Patient and brave and true,
Who trusted and fought and lived and died
For the Lord they loved and knew.
And one was a doctor, and one was a queen,
And one was a shepherdess on the green:
They were all of them saints of God and I mean,
God helping, to be one too.

They loved their Lord so dear, so dear,
 And his love made them strong;
And they followed the right, for Jesus' sake,
The whole of their good lives long.
And one was a soldier, and one was a priest,
And one was slain by a fierce wild beast:
And there's not any reason—no, not the least—
Why I shouldn't be one too.

They lived not only in ages past,
There are hundreds of thousands still,
The world is bright with joyous saints

Who live to do Jesus' will.
You can meet them in school, or in lanes, or at sea,
In church, or in trains, or in shops, or at tea,
For the saints of God are just folk like me,
And I mean to be one too.

As I sang these familiar words, I considered that at that moment, Grandmother, too, was indeed a saint of God.

The congregation quickly filed out of the church after the hymn. I'm not sure how many of the communicants greeted Dr. Taylor since my grandmother, Dr. Washington, and I were the last to leave. Outside the church, there were no words spoken among us. Dr. Washington just smiled at my grandmother, put on his hat, and started walking back down Windsor Avenue to the gates of St. George's. Grandmother and I got into the car and drove home, where we had two glasses of sherry each.

Joe

We were there early, before they even opened the doors. It was the Thursday before school was to begin and my mother had brought me to the clinic for the physical examination required by the state of all its students. When they unlocked the front door at 8:00, we walked to the cubicle that housed the receptionist and Mother gave her my name. I looked at the signs that flanked the plate-glass window. The sign on the left read "White," the one on the right "Colored." Beneath the lettering were arrows pointing in opposite directions. We stepped into the room on the right and settled into cracked leather seats. There were a couple of badly yellowed prints on the wall and an anemic plant of some kind on a stand in the corner. The pock-marked coffee table held three-year-old copies of "Life," "National Geographic," "Redbook," and "Sports Illustrated." I leafed through a worn issue of "Sports Illustrated" and its cover story of the Pirates' improbable victory over the Yankees in the 1960 World Series. Mother had brought some knitting and settled down to that task. A veteran waiter, she had come prepared. She knew that being first at the clinic bore no connection to when we would actually be seen. She planned on utilizing her time and as she began her work, the clicking of her needles seemed to punctuate my own apprehension.

I was not apprehensive about seeing the doctor; I knew that this was a basic eye, ears, and throat kind of check-up. What I was a nervous about was the prospect of school. Not because I would be attending a school new to me—we had moved several times in my twelve years and I generally acclimated myself well to new surroundings. I found it easy to concentrate on school in those situations and let the friendships develop as they might. But I was concerned about being surrounded by white children because I had never gone to an integrated school in my life. I didn't fear whites in any way, foolishly believing in my own infallibility, but I was curious about them and often wondered why they behaved the way they did. Because, as I thought about it, their behavior, as described to me by my parents, was indeed very curious. My father said one of two attitudes would prevail when I walked into Robert E. Lee Elementary the next Monday. It was possible that I would be totally ignored, that people would not recognize my presence at all so that I would wonder if in fact I might be invisible. Or, he said with more gravity, they might choose to antagonize me, to break me down by calling me names—"nigger" or worse. They might seek to goad me into fights by tripping me or spitting on me. And the worst part of all, he insisted, was that there would be no one there to help me. He said I couldn't count on someone in a position of responsibility to react expediently when I was the one that needed assistance. It was this uncertainty that bothered me, that had caused me to lie awake the last few nights and wonder what it would be like to not have any control over those things that affected me.

I was still amazed by how rapidly events unfolded those two weeks prior to school. One day my life was secure, if lonely, the next it was chaotic. My father raised the subject of school one night at dinner. It seems that three gentlemen from the "Committee for Social Change" had visited him that day in his office. The three representatives of the Committee were Alvin Edwards, pastor of the A. M. E. church, Rodney Buruss, owner of Rose Creek Barber Shop, and James McClenney, Dean of Students at St. George's. All three men were widely respected in the local colored community and had deep roots there. Mr. McClenney's involvement in the effort was a calculated one because the college, dependent as it was on the generosity of others, took no official position on desegregation. Apparently, the Committee had targeted me as a candidate to integrate the schools once that decision had been made and assurances of support given. As was explained to my father, I was a good choice for this effort because I was new to the area and had experienced unsettled situations before. Also, they appealed to Daddy's pride in me by insisting that the Committee wished to engage only the brightest and most conscientious children for this effort. I was the only boy in the group of five, and with Regina Lewis, daughter of another St. George's professor, the oldest of the children. The Committee apparently felt that girls might not be subject to the threat of physical abuse the way boys would and that the younger white children would not be as vituperative as their older schoolmates. The Committee was, of course, wrong on both counts. Mr. McClenney's daughter, Melanie, a rising fourth-grader was to be one of the girls involved. The other two were sisters, Ruth and Diane Thompson, daughters of the owner of Bluestone's Negro funeral parlor.

My father told his visitors that we would talk about it that night at dinner and we did. I have always been thankful for the way my parents involved me in all family decisions. I was never sent out of the room so that the adults could discuss some matter that involved all of us. For example, we had, as a family, discussed my father's notion to attend Emmanuel Episcopal Church on the Sunday of the Labor Day weekend. We agreed that Daddy should not force the issue and that the gesture would be a one-time occurrence. We knew, in fact, that subsequent Sundays would find "ushers" outside the church during the entire service to discourage my father or any other undesirables from entering the sanctuary. But we concurred with him that perhaps it was time to send a message, time to let the white people of Bluestone know that there were other people who believed that some things needed to be changed. My parents respected my opinion—after all, they had raised me—and they expected me to offer it freely. I didn't always adhere to these expectations because I learned at an early age that there are advantages to keeping your own counsel.

No one spoke for several moments after Daddy finished describing the Committee's "offer." We were each, I guess, trying to absorb and sift through the information, looking at it from every possible selfish angle. Finally, Daddy asked, "What do you think, Joe?"

Mother answered before I could. "I don't know, Herbert. The whole idea frightens me."

"Of course it does. It frightens me, too. But look at it this way. We want the best possible education for Joe, don't we? And the elementary school, even with a depleted staff, will be far better than the Negro school with its outdated books and equipment. Also, it's not like Joe will be leaving any friends behind by going to Lee. And finally, Lee is just a few blocks away so that if anything did happen we could be right there."

My mother nodded at Daddy's reasoning and offered no further protests. It's funny, but for some reason during their exchange, I kept thinking of Dallas and the visit Daddy and I had paid her the previous week. That visit had gnawed at me for days. It was like I was embarrassed to be there, embarrassed to intrude upon one who had so little, ill at ease, perhaps, with what I knew to be my own relative comfort. And then I was embarrassed for being so selfish, for perceiving the world through the filter of my own experience. We took her some groceries—Daddy had even bought her a ham—and stayed well beyond the time I felt such an occasion dictated. And I couldn't get over how Daddy seemed so at home in Dallas' threadbare house. Things I noticed with disbelief, even revulsion, did not distract him. Or if they did, he never indicated it. He and Dallas talked a good hour, recalling mutual acquaintances or reminiscing about bygone places and events. Once Daddy got her going she wouldn't hardly slow down to breathe although her voice seemed fragile from disuse. I know she was touched by our attention, but Daddy was touched, too. When he finally got up to leave, he leaned over and kissed her on her leathery cheek.

For some reason now, in the security of our dining room, I was connecting Dallas with the subject of that night's discussion. I'm not sure why I made that connection, but it existed nonetheless. I felt that if I did not go to Lee, I would somehow be abdicating my responsibility to Dallas. The notion seemed absurd on many levels. There was little, I thought, that related my circumstances to those of the old lady. But I kept seeing that bony face, with its cataractal eyes and wisps of chin hair and I knew what I had to do.

"I'm going," I said suddenly to my parents.

Daddy and Mother looked at me, then at each other, and then at me again.

"I'm proud to hear you say so, son," said Daddy.

In the waiting room, Mother's knitting needles clicked on. She paused occasionally when we heard the front door open and the subsequent exchange at the receptionist's window. From time to time we could hear a name called on the other side and footsteps retreating down the corridor to one of the examining rooms, even though those called had come to the clinic after our own arrival.

"You're sure you want to do this?" my mother asked me.

"Everyone has to get a check-up," I answered.

"You know what I mean."

I did. "Yes ma'am. I want to."

"Well, we've got to get you some new clothes. We'll go over to Bloom Brothers once we're done here—if we're ever done here. We can't have you looking like some stray cat."

I had never looked like a "stray cat" in my life and she knew it. She wouldn't allow it. She wouldn't let me leave the house without an inspection. More often than not she'd proclaim, "You're not going out of this house looking like that. Somebody saw you dressed like that might believe your mother didn't know any better. Go upstairs and put on something respectable."

I never protested—it did no good to do so—even though Mother's idea of respectable differed vastly from my own. The previous Saturday, for example, she had insisted I wear a tie went I went to the matinee with Regina Lewis, the daughter of one of Daddy's colleagues at St. George's. I wasn't keen about this "date" to begin with; the whole affair had been arranged by our respective fathers and was meant to be a welcoming gesture on the part of the Lewis family. My uneasiness about the occasion was not helped by my mother dictating the clothes I must wear. I tried to reason with her—it was an afternoon show, for goodness sake, and I could practically guarantee I would be the only one there with a tie on. I even beseeched Daddy to intervene on my behalf, but he wisely declined. He did remind me to use the bathroom before leaving the house because, as we all knew, there might not be a restroom at the theater I could use.

Mr. Lewis and Regina came to our house to pick me up and he delivered us in time for the 2:30 show at the State Theater on Main Street. Now the State Theater had definitely seen better days and, in fact, it wouldn't be long before television and integration conspired to close its doors forever. Then, however, it, like many public buildings in Bluestone, was a segregated facility. Regina bought our tickets at the window and we walked around to the side of the building to the "Colored" entrance. The door was propped open and we walked up the stairs to the balcony where the usher, some Negro boy I did not know, took our tickets. The balcony was definitely an afterthought in the construction of the theater and it was easy to imagine that the original projection room and office space had been hastily converted in the wake of "separate, but equal" court rulings.

The floor was sticky with the residue of littered candy and as we settled into our seats, they loudly protested. We had chosen to sit in the balcony's front row, but even so, there seemed to be a great chasm between us and the screen. We were not so far removed, however, that I couldn't notice two adhesive tape patches on that large white surface.

It seems incredible to me now, but the movie we had come to see was "Gone With the Wind." And even though the film was twenty-five years old, this was the first time it had ever run in Bluestone. Because of the Civil War Centennial, local interest in that conflict was high—not that the events of those tumultuous years were ever too far removed from the collective conscience of the town's white populous. I had heard that most of these people had already seen the film, taking, for example, family excursions to Richmond and the grand Lowe's Theater during one of the epic's frequent screenings in the Capital of the Confederacy. Even so, Mr. Hicks, the proprietor of the State, had enthusiastically promoted the movie. "Opening Night" had been the previous Saturday and half-price admission was offered to anyone who came to the theater in "antebellum attire." Apparently, several women had shown up in their grandmother's ball gowns and a couple of the gentlemen turned out with ancestral swords strapped to their sides.

Regina and I exchanged a few pleasantries as we waited for the movie to begin. She asked me how I was liking St. George's, what my last home had been like, that sort of thing. The questions seemed well-rehearsed as if she had already considered that we might not really have anything to talk about and she wanted to do her best to avoid any uncomfortable silences. She offered opinions on the other children of St. George's and while she obviously did not approve of some of her compatriots, her comments were never mean-spirited. In fact, she managed to say something positive about everyone and I admired her for it.

Sitting in the dimly illuminated theater, I slowly became conscious of this female form beside me. I studied her carefully. She had on a pink and white striped dress, white knee socks and what appeared to be new saddle oxfords. Her hair was short and straight and on the back of her neck I could see faint traces of talcum powder. Her budding breasts, reminded me that this girl was on her way to becoming a woman, an intriguing concept that engendered in my body vague perceptible stirrings. When the lights were finally extinguished, I was suddenly less resistant to the whole notion of this forced outing. I fumbled around for Regina's hand during the previews, but she successfully rebuffed me, indoctrinating me into that time-honored ritual I would come to know well during the next few years. Anyway, it was a long movie, I assured myself. Maybe later.

Just as the feature was beginning, some boy at the end of the row surreptitiously tossed a piece of crushed ice from his drink at those sitting below. Two heads immediately whipped around and stared in our direction. The light emanating from the screen allowed me to clearly see the two victims, Will and Drew. I doubt they could see us distinctly—black faces against a dark background—but I had the definite impression that their gaze was fixed on me. After a few agonizingly slow seconds, they turned back around. The boy threw no more ice, not willing, I imagine, to risk censure from the adults in the balcony or to further antagonize those below.

Of course, the movie offended me, dedicated as it was to glorifying an era and a way of life I found repugnant. Mother and Daddy had relayed to me the night before the basic premise of the film, but they had not, as I later realized, condemned it. They wanted me to come to my own conclusions which they would happily discuss with me when I indicated I was interested in doing so. I remember the unflinching devotion of the slaves at Tara and the incongruity of their actions. Did the slaves really behave this way or was this the way the world wanted to believe they behaved? I was embarrassed but I couldn't tell exactly why. Was it the stereotypical depiction of the blacks in the film or my own uncertainty about what was real and what was not? I could not articulate my reservations at the time, but I was distinctly aware of how uncomfortable I was throughout the movie.

Regina was another story. She sniffled and wept throughout—the death of Mr. O'Hara, the fall of Atlanta, poor Melanie's demise—and even laughed with the others when Butterfly McQueen proclaimed, "I don't know nothing about birthing no babies, Miz Scarlett." Regina clutched the arms of her seat and any romantic fantasies I might have entertained dissipated as quickly as Tara itself.

Mr. Lewis was waiting for us when the movie ended and the ride home was consumed by his daughter's recapitulation of the story. They dropped me off at the house, where I ran upstairs to my room, pulled off my tie, and stretched out on the bed with my book on Willie Mays. Soon I was back in a world I knew to be secure and inviolate.

We had been at the clinic an hour and a half when the nurse finally called my name. "I'll wait for you here," my mother said as I got up to follow the nurse down the hall. She pointed me into one of the examining rooms. "Strip down to your underwear. Dr. Butler will see you in a minute," she said and closed the door behind her. The room was stark, sparsely furnished with an examining table, swivel chair, sink, medicine cabinet, and a gleaming metal trash can in the corner. Numerous diplomas and certificates were arrayed on the wall and on the back of the door was a hook where I hung my shirt and pants. I neatly folded my socks and placed them carefully in my shoes at the foot of the examining table. I hopped up on the table, wrinkling the thick white paper as I sat, and began counting the holes in the acoustical tile ceiling. I was trying to distract myself because I was suddenly anxious sitting with no clothes on in this strange room. I tried to think morbid thoughts, car wrecks and the like, for one of my greatest fears at that age was getting an erection at an inappropriate moment. I seemed to have no control over the independent mind of my penis and I was mortified to think that I could have an erection when the doctor came in. Of course, consciously concentrating on not being stiff caused a stirring in my briefs. I was just beginning to panic when the door opened and a short, bald-headed man in a white coat walked in.

"I'm Dr. Butler, Joe," he said, offering me his hand.

Surprised, I extended my own, "Nice to meet you," I said.

"Well," he said, "let's check things out, shall we?" And with that he began his examination. He looked in my ears, my eyes, checked my blood pressure, heart, and lungs. He tapped on my knee with his hammer and, as I feared, pulled down my briefs, felt me, and said, "Cough." He recorded my height and weight and asked me questions about childhood illnesses and immunizations. He was businesslike, but convivial throughout the examination, during which he managed to ask me about my family, my former home, my hobbies. He put me at ease immediately and I had the impression he was interested in what I had to say. My perception was undoubtedly abetted by his appearance. Dr. Butler was one of the least imposing figures I had ever encountered. He was shorter than I and his bald head with its fringe of grey hair gave him an elfish look.

He finished his examination and instructed me to get dressed, which I did while he sat in the chair and jotted notes on the clipboard in his hand. When I sat down again he looked up at me and announced that I was in good health.

"You're a little thinner than I'd like to see," he continued, "but I don't think it's anything to worry about. Unless you are going out for football."

"No sir. I'm a baseball player," I said and I was surprised by the assertiveness of my voice.

"Is that right? I'm a Giants fan myself."

"Me too," I almost shouted.

"Good for you. I grew up in New York and my dad used to take me to the Polo Grounds when I was a boy." He paused. "I sure did hate to see them move to California. Ah well, you can't stop progress, can you, Joe?" he asked with a wink.

"No sir."

He stood up, tore a sheet of paper from the pad on the clipboard and handed it to me.

"It was nice to meet you, Joe. You take this form to school with you next week. It certifies that you have had a check-up and were found to be in good health. And Joe," he added, "take good care of yourself, you hear?"

"Yes sir," I muttered, curious about the sober tone of his last remark.

We shook hands and he opened the door for me. With a hand on my shoulder, he pointed me back toward the waiting room where Mother gathered her knitting and stuffed it into her bag. "A-O-K," I said, showing her the piece of paper Dr. Butler had given me. We walked to the receptionist's window and while Mother paid for the examination, I glanced over into the Whites' waiting room. Will and his mother were sitting there, alone. They didn't see me, but as Mother and I turned to leave, I stuck my head into the room. "Hey," I said. They both looked up at me and I returned Will's inquisitive stare. "See you Monday," I said as Mother grabbed me by the elbow and led me out the front door into the bright sunshine.

Will

Robert E. Lee Elementary School was a large, two-story brick structure situated on a hill three blocks from my home. The school was surrounded by ancient oak trees that managed to keep the building cool, even on the hottest of days. Below the school was an asphalt playground and the two were connected by three tiers of stone steps. I had fallen on these steps in the first grade and the three stitches I received left a vestigal scar on my chin. The interior of the school featured a grand central staircase where the entire student body assembled at Christmas to sing carols. The classrooms' wooden floors smelled of disinfectant every morning, thanks to Bynum's evening labors, and they groaned audibly whenever anyone walked across the uniformly wide boards. The ten foot high ceilings were tangled with cobwebs—like some old man's beard—in the corners where they intersected with the walls.

The classrooms' large leaded windows were open even in winter since the steam-fueled radiators noisily churned out a stifling envelope of heat. I remember the contrasting sensations of sharpening my pencil at the windowsill, breathing the cold air and cranking the handle, each revolution bringing my knuckles precariously close to the frosted canted glass, while waves of

71

warmth flushed my body.

In the classrooms of the primary grades, desks were bolted together on runners in uniform rows, the back of one seat becoming the hinged table of the desk behind it. Above each of the chalkboards lay a green border, the letters of the alphabet written in impeccable cursive. The chalkboards were flanked by small American flags and framed reproductions of Charles Wilson Peale's portrait of George Washington. First in war, first in peace, first in the hearts of his countrymen. These classrooms, two for each grade, were downstairs, as were the principal's office and the lunchroom.

The fourth, fifth, sixth, and seventh grades were upstairs. Again, there were two classrooms for each grade, one for students who read at or above grade level, the other for children who did not. In the sixth and seventh grades, to prepare us for the vagaries of high school, we were exposed to different teachers during the course of the day. There was Mrs. Nelson, the young and enthusiastic English teacher who taught only three years before she did what was expected of her and started having babies. Mrs. Clark taught arithmetic in a clear and precise manner, the last time in my academic career that I seemed to understand the world of mathematics. The science teacher was Mrs. Blick, a well-intentioned lady from out in the county who was, unfortunately, as dry as the brittle leaves that clung to the oak trees in November. Mrs. Doyle, wife of the mayor of Bluestone, taught geography and Virginia history. The teachers rotated among the classrooms of the sixth and seventh grades while we remained cloistered in our respective cells. One period of the day was devoted to either health or music and art, depending on the semester. Health classes were segregated by sex, although there was certainly little discussion of the mysteries of reproduction. Most of the class focused on matters of personal hygiene and the respective roles males and females could expect to play in society. Music and art class was conducted by Mrs. Daniels, wife of the Presbyterian minister, who resigned herself to God's will that she try to engender an appreciation of the finer things in life in the souls of culturally illiterate children.

I was excited by the prospect of being a seventh grader and spending my last year at Robert E. Lee Elementary before moving on to the high school the following fall. There was no middle school or junior high in those days although many parents acknowledged concerns about having eighth graders and twelfth graders in the same facility. But for me, those concerns were a year away and I meant to take full advantage of my "senior" status. As seventh graders we were dismissed first for lunch which gave me five extra minutes to utilize three days a week when I walked home and our maid, Ruth, had a bowl of tomato soup and a grilled cheese sandwich waiting for me. The other two days of the week I took a lunch which I often traded for the school food bought by Mike Rainey. For some reason, he preferred my mother's peanut butter and jelly sandwiches to the hot dogs or, on Fridays, fish sticks offered by the lunchroom. There was a tacit agreement between us and he knew what meals I considered worthy of a swap. We met under one of the oak trees, affected the trade, and sat and talked about baseball and girls. One day in our sixth grade year, Debbie Jones asked us what "fuck" meant and while Mike and I smirked at her naivete, neither of us undertook an explanation because neither of us was sure of the details ourselves.

Being seventh graders also meant that we were undisputed masters of the playground. We chose the teams for kickball and we dictated who could and could not play, a prerogative I fully exercised. There was ample time for these games because every day we were granted two extended recesses, the theory being that play time enervated us of energy that could be negatively channeled in the classroom. On the days I was captain of a kickball team, I excluded the girls from play, excepting, of course, Dean and Brenda Pinchbeck whose ample right leg could generate impressive power when it squarely met the ball.

I awoke early on the morning of the first day of school. I ate my cereal, fed the dog, and brushed my teeth all before I heard anyone else in the family stirring. I was truly excited about the commencement of another school year. Yet I also understood that this opening day would be unlike any I had ever known and that knowledge enhanced my anticipation. Father, Mother, and I had discussed the situation the night before with Father advising me to keep my distance from the colored children. No good could come from being friendly with them, he warned. I was not to be mean in any way; I was just to ignore them. By being friendly, I ran the risk of alienating my friends and the friends of my parents. Mother didn't say much during this discussion, deferring, I suppose, to Father's "understanding of the local situation." The gravity of Father's admonitions alarmed me. Of course I knew the matter of integration was a serious one, yet I was unprepared for my father's somber declarations. I still wanted to believe in the goodness of my fellow man although I admit I was mildly disappointed when I arrived at school and found no assembled protestors. Maybe the images of Central High in Little Rock were still in my mind and I expected shouting hordes of white people and a cordon of National Guardsmen surrounding Robert E. Lee Elementary. The grounds of the school were quiet, however, as was the surrounding neighborhood.

I gathered with my friends—Drew, Mike, Junior—and we loitered on the playground. Ostensibly we talked baseball and whether the Dodgers could hold on to win the pennant. But our discussion was half-hearted at best as each of us let our eyes scan the playground and school for brown faces, Finally, Drew said, "I don't know why the niggers have to go and ruin everything.

Why can't they leave well enough alone?"

It was out in the open now and Junior wasted no time jumping in. "Nobody asked them to come here. Why don't they just stay at their own school?"

"Let one of them get in my way and they'll wish they had," Drew concluded.

We were quiet, then. Of course, being twelve-year-old boys we were used to "talking big," but Drew's words echoed with a sincerity that made me uncomfortable.

When the bell rang, we hurried up the steps to the building, then upstairs to Mrs. Doyle's room. She was our homeroom teacher and it was in this space that we passed the year. Mrs. Doyle had us sit in alphabetical order and as we settled into our desks, we went about the business of turning in completed forms and filling out others. We had been engaged in this tedium for about ten minutes when there was a rap at the door and in walked Mr. Hart, the principal, escorting Joe. Mr. Hart looked ill. His silver hair was rumpled and beads of perspiration clung to his forehead. You could already see sweat stains spreading from the armpits of his white shirt. Joe, on the other hand, seemed collected. His dark trousers were pressed and creased to a razor fine-edge and his white shirt was undisturbed by even the faintest of wrinkles. He wore a black tie and since I still dressed with clip-ons to go to church, I was impressed by the immaculate Windsor knot at Joe's throat.

Mr. Hart spoke. "Mrs. Doyle, this is Joe Washington. He will be joining this class."

"Thank you, Mr. Hart," she replied and with that our principal excused himself and left the room, Mrs. Doyle directed Joe to the empty desk behind Sarah Thomas and I suddenly realized that our teacher's seating plan had the advantage of relegating Joe to the back of the room in perhaps its most inconspicuous spot. I was in the adjacent row and as he walked by I nodded, but if he noticed me he did not acknowledge it.

Mrs. Doyle finished up her administrative chores and assumed her role as our teacher of social studies, the first class of the day. She passed out the Virginia history textbooks we rented for the year and we recorded their numbers and wrapped them with brown book covers. We opened the texts to the first chapter and began reading it orally. It was all about the Virginia Company and Sir Walter Raleigh and what a gentleman he was because he put down his cape over a mud puddle so the Queen wouldn't get her feet wet. And how he had this vision to come to the New World and claim it for England and thus bring Christianity to the savages and honor to his sovereign. It was all familiar territory, of course, because we had studied the same material in fourth grade. And as we went around the room, each reading a paragraph, I wondered what, if anything, would distinguish this year's study.

I counted ahead and was relieved to find my paragraph was a short one which I read with great dispatch when my turn came. Joe's paragraph was detailed, describing the rigors confronting the settlers at Roanoke Island, and I think we were all surprised at the alacrity of his reading. He read with deliberation and his carefully modulated voice echoed the emphases of the text. He followed the punctuation clearly so that the cumulative effect of the words was apparent. I think it was the first time I was exposed to someone my age who understood the nuances of language and who did not feel that reading was a race to be run as quickly as possible. As we began our rounds again, Joe's effortless rendering contrasted sharply with Drew's stumbled efforts, and I could see Drew turning red from the harsh glare of comparison. When the class ended, we had worked our way around to the end of the chapter, the unexplained disappearance of the settlers and the mysterious word "Croatan" found carved in a tree. Mrs. Doyle instructed us to answer the questions at the end of the chapter for homework and she left us to go to the other seventh grade class, comprised largely of the children of laborers for the railroad and the brickyard.

We had four minutes of idle time before the next class would commence with the arrival of Mrs. Clark. We were allowed to get out of our seats but could not leave the room. Mrs. Doyle was barely out the door before Junior, Billy Bledsoe, and a couple of other boys gathered around Drew's desk and were engaged in whispered conversation. Even though I was curious, I did not join them as the looks on their faces meant trouble. They glanced at me once, or so I thought, until I realized they were staring past me at Joe. I turned around in my seat and also gazed at him. His eyes were focused on his history book and he was writing out the answers to the homework questions. I considered speaking to him—I could use the homework assignment as a pretext—but I remembered my father's words and turned back around in my desk. When Mrs. Clark entered, everyone sat down and, with the ringing of the bell, she called roll and began our indoctrination into the mysteries of new math.

The rest of the morning was uneventful as each of us, I think, struggled to find that internal rhythm that would sustain us during the next nine months. I spent much of English class admiring Mrs. Nelson's legs and contemplating what lay at their conjunction. I wondered what she could possibly see in her husband Stanley, ex-high school football star and current tobacco buyer, and consoled myself with the understanding that one day she would undoubtedly leave him and his little pot belly for my undeniable charms. At noon we were dismissed for lunch and I grabbed my brown paper bag from under my desk and headed out the door. Joe was the last to leave the room and as he descended the stairs, Dean and I watched him from the first floor hallway where we had stopped to talk.

"This must be really hard for him," Dean said, "coming to a new school and all." I was surprised by the sympathetic tone of her voice.

"I reckon," I replied as Joe reached the bottom of the stairs and turned down the corridor toward the lunchroom. We had not seen Drew in the shadows behind the stairs but as Joe walked down the short hall, Drew emerged and bumped into him.

"Watch where you're going, boy," Drew shouted. Joe didn't say a word. He tried to sidestep Drew and move on, but Junior and Billy appeared from their hiding place and blocked his way. I was frozen by this scene that was unfolding before me. Fights at school were not uncommon, but scores were invariably settled on the playground. There was no code of behavior for what I was now witnessing. Even though Drew was just inches from Joe's face, I could clearly hear what he said next.

"Just what are you trying to prove anyway?"

"I'm not trying to prove anything," Joe answered calmly. "I just want to eat my lunch."

"Eat your lunch?" Drew echoed. "Why don't you eat this instead?" he said as his closed fist struck Joe full in the face. Joe slumped against the wall and Drew was on him in an instant, riding him to the floor,

"Get him, Drew! Whip his ass!" yelled Junior and Billy as Drew punched furiously at his prone victim. Dean ran to the office and her motion activated me. I joined the ever-thickening cluster that surrounded the bodies on the floor. Joe covered his face with his arms but Drew still boxed him pretty good about the ears. I watched, paralyzed, as Joe tried to protect himself, and I think for the first time in my life I was aware of how it feels like to be totally disappointed in yourself.

Mr. Hart descended on the crowd, his worst nightmare realized, and quickly pulled Drew off of Joe. Joe stood up and we saw the trickle of blood that ran from his nose and disappeared under the collar of his shirt. He accepted the handkerchief Mr. Hart pulled from his back pocket and offered to him.

"What's going on here?" he asked. "Who started this?"

No one answered. Joe looked at me, his eyes never leaving my face so that I had to cast my own eyes to the floor.

"All right," said Mr. Hart. "You boys come with me." He grabbed Drew and Joe by their elbows. "The rest of you go on to lunch."

We dispersed slowly and shuffled our way into the lunchroom. The cafeteria ladies were dishing out Salisbury steak, beets, and chopped kale. I walked over to the table where Dean was sitting, alone. When I sat down across from her, she closed her lunch box, stood up, and went to join Sarah Thomas and Brenda Pinchbeck at a table across the room.

The cafeteria was still buzzing as the kids from the lower grades started to file in. The word was out, you could tell, and everyone was talking excitedly. Mike, who had joined me, claimed to have witnessed the whole fight although I didn't recall seeing him there. He was giving me his version of the event when I noticed the four black girls walk in. They clutched their lunches and timidly moved to an unoccupied table. They sat down and carefully looked about, their eyes wide as a fawn's caught in the headlights of a speeding car, and began nibbling their meals.

When we returned to class, Drew and Joe were conspicuously absent. Of course my curiosity was piqued and I have little recollection of that afternoon's science or art history lesson. Like most of my classmates, I imagine, I was preoccupied with thoughts of our absent peers. However, it was not until after school that I learned their fates from Rickey House, a boy from the other seventh grade class who spent one period a day as an aide in the office. According to Rickey, Drew had been suspended for three days and would not be allowed back in school until

Friday. Rickey said that Mr. Bailey had been furious when he came to pick up his son and, even though he met with Mr. Hart behind the closed door of the principal's office, you could easily hear him shouting while sitting in the reception area. Mr. Bailey seemed to blame Mr. Hart for the whole fiasco and guaranteed that he had not heard the last from him. Dr. Washington had been summoned, too, and despite his son's insistence that he was all right, wanted to take Joe to the doctor's office just to be safe. Joe would be back in school tomorrow, Rickey said.

I was relating these facts to my family that night at dinner when the telephone rang. It was Jim Bailey and from the hall we could hear Father's muted responses.

Yes, he had heard about it and, no, he wasn't sure anything could be done or should be done. All right, he would be willing to talk about it and, yes, he'd come by for a few minutes after dinner. When he sat down again, Father changed the subject, asking my brother for a full report on the high school football team and the prospects for victory in Friday's season opener against Park View. Father excused himself after dinner and later as I prepared for bed, I looked out of the window and saw the driveway still empty.

The next morning Joe was back in school, his lips puffy and his left eye almost swollen shut. We went over our homework in history class and as we reviewed the questions, Joe raised his hand to answer each one. Mrs. Doyle did not call on him, even when he and I were the only ones with upraised arms and I had already responded to others. We launched into the second chapter of the text and towards the end of the class, Mrs. Doyle stopped our reading to announce our first project. We were each to create a poster depicting some facet of life in seventeenth-century Virginia. We would present the posters in class next Thursday and they would be displayed that evening for our parents at Back-to-School Night.

My heart sank at the thought of this assignment. I was not, am not, a creative person by nature and any project requiring that sort of impulse generally resulted in abysmal failure for me. Last year in World History, my rendering of the "fertile crescent" looked like a tangled web of spaghetti. I didn't understand why Mrs. Doyle insisted on these artistic endeavors. Why couldn't we just stick with reading and answering questions, skills at which I excelled? The mere thought of this project made me feel like the time when, at age six, I got lost in the mall in Richmond where Mother had taken me to buy new shoes.

School soon settled into a predictable routine. Everyone, myself included, pretty much ignored Joe, even at recess where he sat on the periphery of our games and looked on in silence. He and the other colored children continued to eat together until Tuesday of the second week when Dean suddenly took her lunch to their table and sat with them. I had gone home for lunch that day but Mike Rainey greeted me with the news upon my return. That afternoon, walking home with Dean, I asked her why she had done such a thing. "I'm just trying to make them feel welcome," she said. "How would you feel if you were one of only five white children in an all Negro school?" End of conversation. I could not argue with her, nor, really, did I want to. I accepted her attitude as just one more indication that my view of the world was subject to forces beyond my control.

Life at home settled into a comfortable routine as well; my brother and sister were consumed by the demands of high school. My brother, a 140 pound split end, had amazed us all by catching the game-winning touchdown against Park View. My sister was a cheerleader, basking in the status that position conferred and they were both heavily engaged in the mysterious world of dating. Father went to work every day and Mother did whatever she did when we were not at home. For the moment, there was no more talk of the situation at Robert E. Lee Elementary.

I walked to school anxiously on the day the posters were due. I had put off my project until the night before, considering and dismissing in turn a number of possibilities. I wanted to do something beyond the minimum, but such inebriate enthusiasm was sobered by my limited artistic abilities. I finally decided to draw a picture of the Susan Constant, the Godspeed, and the Discovery, the three ships that had ferried the original 105 settlers to Jamestown. After all, how difficult could it be to draw some ships and a patch of ocean, I reasoned. I found a picture of the vessels in the textbook and set about duplicating it on posterboard. It only took a few minutes of effort to realize I was in deep water and my spirits soon lost the buoyancy so nobly displayed by Captain Christopher Newport's sturdy ships. I labored on for two hours, trying to keep my vision afloat. When I finished, I was, of course, disappointed at the resulting brown and white blobs on blue background. I quickly printed the names of the ships on the dingy hulls to aid in the identification of my illustration.

As we presented our posters, the responses were predictable. Most of us had been in school together for six years and we could easily guess who would create something visually appealing and who would not. Most of our efforts were greeted with suppressed giggles and Mrs. Doyle valiantly struggled to find an encouraging or complimentary remark as it became clear to her that we had lived up to our own expectations of ourselves and not those she in fact held for us.

Drew, going first, set the tone for the proceedings with his poster of a single green leaf of tobacco, cash crop of Virginia. Dean, always attracted by independent and assertive women, illustrated the legend of Pocahontas saving John Smith's life. Her picture showed Pocahontas kneeling over the prostrate explorer while Chief Powhatan stood in the background. There was little, however, to distinguish one character from the other except for their relative positions in the scenario. Sarah Thomas displayed a portrait of

Virginia Dare, first English child born in the New World.

There was five minutes left in class when Mrs. Doyle called on Joe. He walked to the front of the room, faced us, and unrolled his poster. Along its bottom, in neatly stenciled block letters, were the words, "CROSS-SECTION, INTERIOR OF A SLAVE SHIP." The illustration itself was rendered in fine pen and ink lines, not the large hurried brushstrokes of a magic marker. We were stunned by its exactitude, the beauty of its exquisite detail. The illustration summoned our eyes into the ship's hull, crammed with hundreds of squatting, manacled bodies. These naked forms were stacked like cordwood and even from the back of the room, I could discern looks of anguish and disbelief on their respective faces. Yet each face was different, somehow; each had its own horrific story to tell and it was staggering to contemplate the hours required to create this work. Joe's oral presentation was flawless and in two minutes he detailed how Africans were captured and coerced on board such ships, the alarming number who died in the voyage to the New World. He concluded his well-rehearsed remarks with an overview of the evils of the slave auction.

Throughout, Joe's delivery had been unemotional, but the cumulative effect of his words and poster were numbing. We were all silent as he returned to his seat. We knew, of course, that slaves had been brought to Virginia; as Mrs. Doyle had taught us, their arrival was one of the major events of the "red-letter" year of 1619. However, we had never considered, or been asked to consider, the conditions under which, in time, thousands of slaves travelled to this unknown land. Furthermore, we had been told that slavery, while perhaps unfortunate, was nonetheless a benign institution generally favored by the slaves themselves. Joe's remarks certainly suggested otherwise. I think we were all still trying to absorb what we had seen and heard when Sarah raised her hand.

"Mrs. Doyle," she asked. "Is what he said true?"

Mrs. Doyle scanned our expectant faces. "Yes, Sarah," she said. "I believe it might be."

"Well, how come it ain't in the book, then?" challenged Drew.

"That's a good question. Maybe some people don't want us to know the truth," Mrs. Doyle replied. "Maybe the truth is too hard for us to handle."

And with that observation, Mrs. Doyle was somehow elevated in my estimation. I'm not sure I could explain it, then or now, but her comment seemed to suggest that she was not infallible, that she, like the rest of us, had doubts, fears, anxieties. It was a scary possibility because, as a teacher, we assumed she had an answer to everything. But now, there was at least the suggestion that she was also, in a way, unschooled; she was on our side looking at some vast gulf that separated us and "them."

When the bell rang to end the class, Mrs. Doyle quietly walked out of the room having forgotten to assign us any homework for the next day. There wasn't a sound in the room until four minutes later when Mrs. Clark walked in and told us to get out our math books. We went through some exercises in long division and watched the clock wind its way to recess and the promise of fresh air. I couldn't wait to play kickball; I needed to run and yell, to release this strange gnawing feeling inside of me.

On the playground, Rickey House and I reminded the others that it was our turn to choose sides. Rickey selected Junior first and Drew started to move over behind me, anticipating my accustomed pick. I looked to the edge of the asphalt where Joe, as usual, sat on the stone steps. "Hey, Joe," I shouted. "You want to play?" He nodded. "Come on, you're on my team."

"Are you crazy?" hissed Drew. "You can't choose him."

"I just did."

"Well, I for one ain't going to play with no nigger."

"Suit yourself," I said.

"Come on, Junior," Drew said. "We don't have to put up with this shit."

Junior looked at us all—at Rickey, at me, at Joe who now stood by my side, at Drew. "I reckon I'll play," he said and Drew, disgusted, stomped up the stairs in a huff to school.

I'm not sure what precipitated Junior's decision. I'm fairly sure he was not making a moral stand in any way; perhaps he felt some remorse over his involvement in the fight the previous week. More likely, the lure of kickball outweighed all other considerations, because when you got right down to it, Junior loved a good game more than anything in the world.

And what a game it was. Joe was amazing. It was soon apparent that he was easily the fastest kid in school. He was a flawless fielder who knew the play to make before it had to be made. There was no hesitancy in his efforts, and no wasted motion. It was clear that he was not only physically gifted but mentally intuitive. He was always two plays ahead of us and shyly suggested to me, in my role as captain, strategic possibilities. When, in our last up, he boomed a home run to win the game, it was somehow fitting. We slapped him on the back as he crossed the plate, forgetting, for at least a moment, those things we had been taught and told by our parents.

I congratulated him on his play on the way back to class. That was great how you came through when the pressure was on," I said.

"You call that pressure? Will, you don't know anything about pressure," he replied.

I changed the subject. "Look," I said, "your poster was pretty amazing. Where did you find out all of that stuff?"

"My father told me some; the rest I got from the college library."

"You must have worked on it for hours."

"More like days. But it was worth it, don't you think?" he asked as we entered the classroom and were met by Mrs. Nelson.

Joe continued to join our games during recess the next few days. No one would dare exclude him once we had seen how good he was. Drew even returned to our contests and, to his credit, offered no more challenges to the new accepted order of our pastime.

One Wednesday morning Joe stopped me as we both headed toward homeroom. "The World Series begins today."

"No kidding. The Yankees will win—it's a cinch."

"I wouldn't be so sure." He paused and looked around. "Anyway, listen. My parents said you could come over and watch the game this afternoon, if you wanted to."

It took me a moment to realize that he was inviting me to his house. My first reaction was to quickly scan the hall to make sure no one had overheard us, but we were alone. "Uh, sure, I guess. I mean yes. Thanks. I'll have to go home first and check in with my mom." This was not entirely true. Mother didn't concern herself with my whereabouts until supper time, but it seemed a plausible excuse and it absolved me from getting in the car with Joe and his mother, who was always parked and waiting for her son at the end of each school day.

The rest of that day, I wondered if I was doing the right thing. Suppose my friends found out, my parents? Would they care? Should I care if they did? Did I really want to be friends with Joe outside of school and could I handle all that such a friendship implied? At lunch, I started to tell him I had forgotten I had a dentist appointment that afternoon, but, at the last minute, I changed my mind. I finally figured it had been harder for him to ask me than it had been for me to accept and now that I had, I was determined to go.

I left school in a hurry. I knew Dean would probably want to come to my house and watch the game and I wanted to avoid having to explain to her why she couldn't. I raced home, dumped my books on the bench in the front hall, and told Mother I'd see her later. I ran out the back door and across our field to the woods. I was in a hurry because I didn't want any time to think about what I was doing. I picked my way through the trees, realizing that it had been at least two years since I last walked through the woods to St. George's. When I emerged on the campus, I made my way towards the chapel, behind which, Joe had told me, was the Washingtons' brick home. On the way, I was aware that many of the students crisscrossing the grounds were staring at me. But no one spoke to me and I soon spied Joe's house, identical to the other faculty homes scattered about the campus.

I knocked on the door and Joe opened it, saying, "Come on. It's the fourth inning already. Roseboro just hit a three-run homer."

I followed him into the living room and sat down on the floor beside him, in front of a RCA television hulking in the corner. When Mrs. Washington came in, I stood up and Joe introduced us.

"I'm glad you could come over, Will. Wouldn't you be more comfortable sitting in a chair?"

"No ma'am, the floor's fine. Thank you, though," I added.

"Mom, please," Joe said. "We're trying to watch to the game."

"Sorry, dear. Go right ahead. I'll bring you boys some milk and cookies."

She turned and walked out of the room and I sat back down. Joe looked at me and rolled his eyes and we both understood that being friends with someone meant forgiving him for his parents. As we watched the game, my eyes absorbed all that surrounded me. If I had known at the time what the term was, I would have likened myself to an anthropologist, an observer of a strange and exotic culture. The furnishings in the living room were modern, sleek-looking, and contrasted sharply with the cumbersome antiques that inhabited my house. There were family pictures on the mantle and on the end table by the sofa, a framed photograph of President Kennedy. Through the arched doorway of the dining room I could see a round table and four ladderback chairs. There was a buffet against the far wall and hanging above it a painted plate with the likeness of a dark-skinned Jesus. Everything seemed so clean, so tidy. Even the magazines on the coffee table were deliberately arranged, exhibiting uniform margins.

Mrs. Washington returned with a plate full of homemade chocolate chip cookies and two tall glasses of milk. Joe and I thanked her and as she left the room I realized that she was just a mom, not unlike my own mother or Drew's mother, who simply wanted the best for her child. Of course, that seems fairly obvious, but it was a revelation of sorts, a faint understanding, perhaps, that there was more that bound us all together than separated us.

The game was a classic, although an unhappy one for Yankee fans like myself. Sandy Koufax broke a Series record by striking out fifteen. Joe celebrated each "K" with another cookie although by the seventh inning he was groaning audibly from the effort. When the game was over, I thanked him and his mother, told him I'd see him at school and struck out for home. I figured I'd keep my excursion a secret for awhile. It was not that I was ashamed of where I'd been; I just wasn't sure how my family would react to the news. I didn't think they would really be upset or disappointed, but I wasn't sure. They would definitely be curious, though, and I just wasn't in the mood to be the object of curiosity.

Well, the Dodgers went on to sweep the Series, a miraculous victory to my way of thinking. Mantle had a respectable yet unspectacular four games but he and the other pinstripers could not overcome the pitching strength of Koufax and Don Drysdale. Joe was elated. He was not really a Dodger fan—after all, they were bitter rivals of his beloved Giants—but he was an inveterate National League partisan and the Dodgers, he also reasoned, was the team that had broken baseball's color barrier with the signing of Jackie Robinson.

Joe never missed an opportunity to needle me during the next couple of weeks at school. You see, Joe was accepted now, although within the strict parameters of the school environment. He had proved his athletic powers and in the opinion of my peers and myself, his skills were indeed admirable. He was respected in the classroom as well. He had displaced me as the best student in our class. Although our grades were comparable, Joe succeeded because he loved learning; I succeeded because it was what others expected of me and I, in fact, expected of myself. The teachers soon learned that Joe was an infallible resource, someone who would know the answer to every question they posed thus validating the notion that they must be doing something right after all. Outside of school, our routines were unchanged and I did not visit Joe's home again or reciprocate by asking him to mine.

It was late November, on a glorious Indian summer-like day, that history was made at Robert E. Lee Elementary. There was an extended recess after lunch so that we could run, jump, push and pull ourselves in an attempt to qualify for the President's Physical Fitness Award. President Kennedy had challenged the nation's young people to become strong and fit and we were determined to meet that challenge. The sixth and seventh graders were sent off by homerooms to various parts of the playground where our teachers were to run us through a number of exercises and record the results. We were confident as we began, sure that the youth of Bluestone, Virginia, could stack up against our contemporaries in any other community of the nation. But as we began our efforts, we soon realized that some of the standards were more difficult than we first imagined. I conquered the long jump and the standing broad jump with ease, but, despite the exhortations of my classmates, could not muster the strength required for that one final chin-up to match the number deemed appropriate for my age. Drew surpassed this requisite number but his time in the 800 yard run was half a minute too slow. He blamed his failure on his shoes, new P. F. Flyers that were "not broken in, yet." Others in the class faced similar failures and as we independently worked through the events, a collective sense of gloom seemed to invade us. Only Joe exceeded each of the requirements and as he approached his last event, the 800 yard run, we all stopped to watch him. When Mrs. Doyle shouted "Go!", Joe sped off for the first of the four laps around the asphalt playground. He was incredible to watch, his long legs effortlessly chewing up the yards of black pavement, his arms keeping perfect rhythm. His head was so still it seemed almost disembodied, and his eyes never stopped focusing straight ahead. As he passed us once, twice, and then three times, his breathing was easy and regular. We cheered him on and as he rounded the far corner for the final stretch, his pace perceptibly quickened. He crossed the chalked finish line, Mrs. Doyle clicked the stop watch, and we gathered around to see the time. Joe had beat the standard by an astonishing eighteen seconds. He was still not panting and we slapped him on the back. We all felt enhanced, I think, by his triumph and were ennobled by the knowledge that there would be at least one Presidential Fitness award winner from Bluestone that year.

We returned to the building, happy for Joe and happy that science class, because of the long recess, would be abbreviated. We trooped upstairs to the classroom and took our seats. Mrs. Blick waited for us to settle down and when we did, we became aware that something was troubling her. Her face, more somber than usual, was pale, although her eyes appeared red and puffy. We were quiet; we knew something was not right and our spirits deflated like a balloon with a slow leak.

"Children," she said, "I have some sad news." She paused and looked at each of us in turn. "President Kennedy has been shot in Dallas. He was taken to a hospital where he died in surgery. School will be closing in a few minutes so that you may all go home to be with your families."

We waited for her to say more, to say something else that would somehow contradict the grave news she had just delivered to us. But Mrs. Blick sat down and looked past our heads at the fluffy white clouds that floated past the windows.

We did not know how to react, how to respond to this tragedy. I think my classmates, like me, were sad, and I thought of his beautiful wife and two young children. But mostly, we were confused. How could this have happened? And why would anyone want to kill the President? Kennedy certainly was not a popular figure in Bluestone, having finished third in the local returns behind Nixon and Dixiecrat Strom Thurmond, but he was respected. And we were also confused because none of us had ever had to publicly confront tragedy. As self-conscious adolescents, we did not know how to respond in a room full of other people. Mostly, I think, we stared at the floor in what we deemed to be an appropriate gesture. Some of us thought selfish thoughts, how to take advantage of an unplanned free afternoon, a rare gift.

As we waited for the dismissal bell, I heard from stifled gasps, suppressed breathless sobs behind me. I turned around and saw Joe with his head buried in his arms on the desk. He must have sensed that I was gazing at him, for he suddenly lifted his head in my direction. His wide eyes met mine and I saw big, soft tears flowing freely down his brown face.

1968

Joe

It was a Thursday night, and we didn't hear the news until Dean McClenney called Daddy sometime shortly after 10 o'clock. Of course, in some ways, news of this nature was not unexpected, but that knowledge did not diminish our shock. We turned on the television and watched the first sketchy reports from the Memphis hotel. There was a lot of confusion at the scene, but one fact was indisputable: Dr. Martin Luther King, Jr, was dead. Who had shot him was unclear, but, really, that didn't matter. It could have been anyone and we knew that, just like it could have been anyone who killed Emmitt Till, Medgar Evers, or four little girls in a church in Birmingham. It could have been the man who pumps your gas, does your dry cleaning, or from whom you buy groceries. It could have been any one of the millions of people, white people, who still believed I was less of a human being because my skin was not the same color as theirs. Mother cried and Daddy asked us to join him in prayer, but I don't think his heart was really in it. His words seemed hollow and perfunctory, inadequate for that which they were intended. We finally shuffled off to bed around 1:00 a. m. when the networks shut down for the night, but I don't think any of us actually slept. Twice during the interminable hours until daylight, I heard

Daddy pacing about the house. I wanted to get up and go to him, but something held me back. I think I knew he preferred to be alone and I did not want to force him to have to talk at a time when articulation seemed so difficult.

We were all groggy in the morning, and we absorbed the newspaper in silence. There was not much to say, after all, just meaningless platitudes and clichés that were best not said. I wanted to stay home from school, but Mother wouldn't hear of it. Her method of dealing with grief was to go about your routine just as if nothing had happened. But something had happened, and I knew there would be precious little in my daily ritual to comfort me.

I was a junior at Bluestone High School where full integration was still a year away. Maybe ten percent of the students there were black, children of merchants, preachers, and teachers— what amounted to the "upper class" of the black community. The sons and daughters of the laborers, domestics, and field hands still attended the all-black high school where equality and opportunity were just terms discussed in history class.

I had done well at Bluestone High, home of the Barons. I was ranked near the top of my class, played on the baseball team, and was accepted as much as any black person can be by an overwhelmingly white environment. It was like I was a strange virus—a virus with no known cure—that had invaded a healthy body. Initially, the body tried to reject the virus, to evacuate it, but over time it had come to accept the foreign substance and now was somehow immune to it. There were occasional flare-ups, but, for the most part, the body had learned to coexist with the illness. In some ways the school seemed to take a perverse pride in my presence and in the presence of my black friends. You could almost hear a collective, "Well, they're niggers, but they're our niggers." I sometimes felt like I was the good slave that master treated with benevolence, a walking, breathing testimony to the virtues of an enlightened attitude. As long as I knew my place, didn't forget I was a slave and made sure I used the back door. Or maybe I was like one of those early black actors, whose only film roles involved shuffling feet, scratching heads, and saying, "Yassuh, Boss." The kind of character who was regarded with affection, as long as his behavior fit neatly into a mold cast by those who didn't know him.

Sometimes I could not escape the feeling that I was a school mascot of sorts, an accepted and coddled component of the school environment, but a component that is nonetheless anonymous behind its mask and costume. I remember my freshman year when I made the baseball team. I was the only freshman on the varsity until late in the season when Will was brought up from JV because of injuries to two of our starters. It was our first game of the season, and I really did not know my teammates, juniors and seniors who were already at the high school when I first came to Robert E. Lee Elementary. It was an away game and on the bus ride I sat alone and no one talked to me. I knew they resented me because the coach had already indicated I would start at shortstop, displacing a senior who was very popular but extremely vulnerable to curve balls.

When we took infield practice before the game, I was conscious of the stares from the opposing players, and a quick glance to the stands confirmed I was the only black person in the vicinity. I batted leadoff and I had hardly dug in at the plate when the first pitch came sailing at my head. I hit the dirt, got up, and brushed myself off. I looked at the pitcher who leered at me from behind his scraggly mustache. "Okay," I thought, "he has sent me his message, and I have received it. Now we can play."

I stepped back into the batter's box and again was sent sprawling by a pitch aimed at my head. I looked at the umpire from the ground, figuring he would issue the pitcher a warning, but he didn't say a word. In the stands, a few of the locals were chuckling and my dugout seemed strangely silent. My coach mouthed a couple of obligatory protests towards the umpire, but it did not seem to me there was much conviction in his voice. Twice more I warily stepped to the plate and twice more I collapsed in the dust. I bailed out so quickly I felt I resembled a house of cards whose foundation has been suddenly yanked away. After the fourth pitch, I got up, tossed my bat towards the dugout and trotted down to first base, spitting the dirt out of my mouth.

I took my lead off first as Billy Howard, our center fielder, stepped in at the plate. I was gone on the first pitch and my slide easily beat the catcher's throw, a fact which did not prevent the shortstop from slamming his glove to my thigh when the ball arrived. Billy grounded to the second baseman and I advanced to third, and when Danny Stinnie followed with a fly to short right field, I tagged up and slid home with the game's first run. Coach tried to look nonchalant, but I could tell he was excited. He already knew I could hit and field, but for the first time he had a glimpse of what speed and savvy could do.

We won the game easily, and I had two doubles and a single in four other at bats. I played a steady shortstop and even tagged out an opponent with the hidden ball trick after he had doubled to left. It was perfect and after the game on the bus ride home, my teammates congratulated me and a few even patted me on the back with gestures of approbation. But I never really felt a part of things. Tolerated, maybe, but never totally welcome. When, at the end of the season, Danny had a team party at his house, I was not asked to attend. Even Will, who professed to all I was his friend, never fully acknowledged me in front of others.

I was not even invited last year to his sixteenth birthday, a party attended by everyone who had ever even tangentially known the honoree. Will told me later that he had wanted me to come and his parents wouldn't allow it and I understood, didn't I? Yeah, I understood; I understood that friendship was just a term to be uttered when convenient. There was no substance or sacrifice involved. I guess I shouldn't be too hard on Will; who knows how I might have acted under similar circumstances? I mean it was the biggest party in Bluestone in years and who could turn his back on that, after all?

I know the party was huge because I witnessed it from the cover of the woods behind Will's house. I felt weird looking on from behind the trees like I did when I had watched his summer afternoon baseball games, but I guess I was angry and curious after all.

Over the back yard was a huge tent, borrowed from Jimmy Harlowe, the auctioneer, with Japanese lanterns hanging from the posts that supported the canvas. There was a dance floor under the tent and a small bandstand at one end where played Blue Max, recruited all the way from Roanoke Rapids. The food was ample and Freeman Morris, the security guard at the college, was steadily carving the roast beef and trying not to stain his starched white coat.

It was a pretty boisterous scene and a testimony to the Rawlings' status in the community that the neighbors didn't complain. I mean I could hear Blue Max blasting "Magic Carpet Ride" all the way over at my house. The band was between sets, and I was just about to leave when a car with a wildly honking horn pulled into the driveway. It was a brand new Mustang and as Mr. Rawlings stepped out from the driver's seat, he put his arm around his son and began singing "Happy Birthday." All the guests joined in and then clapped like crazy, pleased with themselves for being rich, white, and secure in their vision of the world. It was more than I could take, and I stole back through the woods sorry I had ever come. Sure, you could say I was jealous and maybe I was, but I think it was more than that, really. I was somehow offended by the smugness of the whole event, the sense of "let's be glad for who we are" that seemed to permeate the evening. It was all too self-congratulatory in a way, and I'm sure Will was confused the next Monday at school when I declined his innocent request to go out to the parking lot at lunch to see his new car.

When I got to school the day after Dr. King's assassination, it was like nothing had happened. I knew the flag wouldn't be at half mast or anything like that, but I guess I did expect some acknowledgement of the event at least. Maybe the principal would come over the intercom and ask us to join him in a moment of silence. Maybe in American History class we would suspend our discussion of World War II to remember Dr. King's contributions to society. Maybe there would even be a special assembly to pay tribute to the slain leader. Of course, I was sadly deluded and as my black friends and I huddled before homeroom, we knew there would be little to distinguish this day from any other at Bluestone High School.

There were some subtle differences, however. That morning as I walked to first period class, I was occasionally greeted with bits of conversation I was meant to overhear. Things like, "Yeah, they got him all right" or "That's one less nigger to worry about." When I saw Will outside of the classroom, he just nodded and looked down as he walked past me to take his seat.

As the day progressed, I looked forward to sixth period and English class. The teacher, Mr. Martin, was just a year out of college and the closest thing Bluestone High School had to someone with a social conscience. I liked him and so did my classmates, once they figured out he was immune to the ritualistic abuse by which all new teachers are tested. He had proved his mettle and had even managed to imbue with energy Longfellow, Holmes, Whittier, and all those other dead white poets. Once he had the temerity to bring to class copies of Langston Hughes's

"Theme for English B." The poem wasn't in the textbook; the 40s vintage anthology had no works by black authors, unless you want to count the three examples of "Negro Spirituals" penned by "Anonymous."

I remember my excitement the day Mr. Martin passed out the copies of Hughes' poem. I was familiar with Hughes—my father made sure of that—but could practically guarantee that none of my classmates had ever heard of him. I remember the strange thrill I felt as Mr. Martin read the poem and how I practically held my breath at "Sometimes perhaps you don't want to be a part of me. / Nor do I want to be a part of you. / But we are, that's true!"

It's pretty hard to explain. I mean the poem is tame by Hughes' standards—he even refers to himself as "colored," for God's sake—but I considered Mr. Martin's action a bold move, nonetheless. I guess it was the whole sense of illicitness about his effort. He had deviated from the textbook, specifically altered the course of study to include a black writer. There was a delicious quality to it, like eating a second piece of pie because it's just so damn good even though you know you're already full.

I thought if anyone would comment on Dr. King's death, then, it would be Mr. Martin. He often talked of current events in class and he had even done a media study unit with us where we were required to make conclusions about point of view from watching television news and reading editorials. But Mr. Martin stuck to his lesson—how to write the five-pararagraph essay—and his demeanor seemed to suggest that he would not sanction any discussion of that which did not pertain to thesis statements and how to support them. I was disappointed, of course, and felt more alone then than at any other time in my years of high school. When the bell rang, we gathered our books to leave. I was just about out the door when Mr. Martin asked, "Joe, you got a minute?"

I stopped and hung back until everyone had cleared the room. Mr. Martin walked over and put his hand on my shoulder. "Joe," he said, "I'm really sorry about Dr, King. It's terrible; I still can't believe it; I feel like I'm in a state of shock. Are you okay?" He searched my eyes for an answer, but I just shrugged and avoided his gaze. I guess I was mad at him in some way, angry because he had not acknowledged his role in the commission of a public sin. He was a white man after all, and like all white men, I felt he should bear some responsibility for Dr. King's murder. It was unfair of me, but I had wanted some visible penance from him in class and when none was forthcoming, I was disappointed. He reminded me of Rev. Dimmesdale from *The Scarlet Letter*, a book he had patiently taught us earlier in the year. Like Dimmesdale, Mr. Martin had not the courage to admit his guilt and Pearl's admonition of her father, "Thou vast not bold! Thou vast not true!" now seemed applicable to my English teacher as well.

He withdrew his hand when I did not further respond to his entreaty. "Well," he said, "I just wanted you to know I was thinking about you. I wanted to say something in class, Joe, but the principal told us this morning not to discuss it. Some sort of nonsense about not wanting to incite a riot."

He smiled at me, and I remember thinking, "I wish he hadn't told me that." This news just made me more disappointed in him, really. It explained his lack of courage, but it did not ameliorate it. I know now that I was too hard on Mr. Martin. He was a good man, doing the best he could. But at the time I guess his best wasn't good enough for me. I needed an unequivocal ally, and it was apparent to me that I wasn't going to find one at Bluestone High School.

There was an awkward silence. I know he wanted me to say, "Thanks," to somehow grant him recognition for his concern, but I just couldn't do it.

"I've got to catch my bus," I finally said.

"Right. Well, listen Joe, you take care of yourself."

I nodded, turned and walked out of the room and the hall to the school entrance and the cordon of yellow buses waiting there.

A memorial service was held that evening at St. George's Chapel. Rev. Estes, the college chaplain, led us in prayer. There was a lot of snuffling and blowing of noses, and I don't think I've ever heard "We Shall Overcome" sung with such feeling. But it wasn't enough, and we all knew it. True, there was a cathartic sense of grief to the service, but there was no opportunity to express disillusionment, to express rage. That's why, after the service, we moved en masse to the Student Union and a hastily assembled forum on "Remembering Dr. King." The forum was moderated by Kenneth Burwell, president of the student body. A light-skinned, intense young man with glasses, Kenneth was widely respected by both the students and the faculty. My father often spoke glowingly of him and his ability as a writer. He was an inspiring speaker who articulated his points with precision.

At the forum, Kenneth insisted that the momentum of Dr. King's work not be lost and insisted that we show the people of Bluestone that we would not forget Dr. King's death. Therefore, he proposed that the college community participate in a silent march through the streets of Bluestone on Monday at noon. It was a stunning idea but even more remarkable was the fact that Dr. Russell, president of the college, assented. Perhaps he feared the reprisal that would surely follow any denial; undoubtedly he sensed the level of helplessness and frustration that permeated the auditorium, but when he stood up to endorse the suggestion, I was shocked. Immediately, my head filled with visions of hundreds of Negroes trooping through the streets of Bluestone. It was an incredible vision to consider and one I had a hard time bringing credence to. The whole scenario seemed too impossible, too surreal, like some dream remembered in vivid detail that is nonetheless divorced from all that you know to be fact. Yet as I sat between my parents in the auditorium, the particulars of the dream began to take definite form. Kenneth formulated a schedule for the march and Dr. Russell assisted by suspending classes for the day. So that by the end of the assembly the details were firmly in place and my spectral visions seemed on the brink of becoming concrete.

The rest of the weekend was lived in anticipation of Monday. We spent time listening to the news reports, commenting on the obligatory messages of condolence from around the world and the details of the funeral to be held Tuesday in Atlanta. I occupied myself those days watching my father. He was angry but he did his best not to show it. I knew his frustration was at odds with his indefatigable optimism. I think he was sad that the world could not escape its own shortcomings, that just when there seemed to be some hope in our collective future, events conspired to remind us how evil we really are. He was distracted and on edge all weekend and all weekend I couldn't escape the feeling that he wanted to talk to me but was somehow scared of what he might say. It was like the time he had given me the "facts of life" talk. I don't recall now how I knew the talk was imminent, but Daddy had spent days then avoiding my eyes and casting quick sidelong glances at me when he thought I wasn't looking. Finally, one evening after dinner, and with encouragement from Mother, he rather formally announced that he would like to see me in the living room. Once there, he stumbled through a well-rehearsed yet awkward recitation about the "birds and bees." What he told me, of course, was not news, but I sat silent so as to not to complicate his task. He dismissed me when he was done and our relationship returned to normal.

Daddy pretty much avoided me those two days following Dr. King's death. I knew he didn't want to have that talk, to have to come to terms with the harshness of the true "facts of life." And I didn't want him to have that talk either. It would be too hard for him to admit to his only child that the world was a place of meanness and despair. So I avoided him, too, and we then managed to survive the weekend without confronting or perpetuating our mutual disillusionment. Monday dawned fresh and clear. Mother's jonquils bloomed in the side yard and the first white buds of the campus dogwood trees emerged. Even the azaleas around President Russell's home showed faint promises of flowering soon. Mother fixed a huge breakfast—sausage, ham, eggs, grits, biscuits, basic stick-to-your-ribs food. She wanted us to have a good meal before we undertook to join the trek though Bluestone, a walk that would take thirty minutes at most. But the copious amount of food she prepared, and the demeanor she displayed in doing so, suggested she was readying us for some extended expedition. Daddy and I ate as much as we could and we all retired to get dressed for the walk. I hesitated for a moment before my closet before pulling down my best suit. I guess I realized that the occasion was one that demanded I look the best I could. The way I figured it, not only were we paying homage to Dr. King, we were also showing the white folk of Bluestone that despite the efforts of their race to suggest otherwise, we were a noble and dignified people. We were, in short, better than they. I waited for Mother and Daddy in the living room and when they joined me, they, too, had on their church clothes. Daddy's black shoes were freshly polished and Mother's white gloves and string of pearls accented her dark dress.

We walked over to chapel and joined the crowd that was forming there. We shook hands with the men, as if we hadn't seen them for a long while, and acknowledged each other in hushed tones. By noon, the size of the crowd was impressive, its numbers rivaled only perhaps by that of the football homecoming game.

The entire student body was there, as were the faculty members and their families and some of the people of the community who had got wind of our plans. There must have been five to six hundred all total. There was very little talking going on and when Kenneth announced it was time, everyone quietly fell into place. Dr. Russell and Dean McClenney joined Kenneth and a couple of the other student leaders at the head of the line. We were a few rows back with Mr. and Mrs. Lewis and Regina.

We walked out of the college entrance and turned left on Windsor Avenue. We reached the corner of Church Street and again turned left past Emmanuel Episcopal Church. I looked over my shoulder at the phalanx of people behind me. I was struck by the paradox of so little noise coming from so many people. We were like low tide, quietly, incessantly lapping at the shore. At the foot of Church Street, we turned right onto Main Street which housed Bluestone's business district. We were in the middle of the road now and our momentum swept us by cars temporarily frozen by our presence. We were like an army of ants marching through an outing of surprised picnickers. Merchants and housewives gathered on the sidewalks to watch us with their immutable faces.

We flowed past the Red & White and the farm supply store where Mr. Rawlings and his employees glared down on us from the loading dock. We turned right at the ABC store where Bradford Dillwyn kept constant vigil. He looked at us from the depths of his alcoholic stupor and was sad, I think, to be so publicly regarded. It was like he was a little boy who's been taken to task for pilfering form he cookie jar one too many times. He suffered a collective yet silent rebuke from the marchers, disappointed that a fellow black man could not rise above his shortcomings on this holiest of days.

It was two short blocks to the gate of the college and the chapel. We milled around for awhile talking, speculating, but, really, there wasn't much to say. The whole event had been strangely unsatisfying in a way, There seemed to be a cathartic sense of accomplishment yet there was a feeling of emptiness as well. What would happen next? To us? Our people? The nation? We didn't know, of course, and I think we all understood the futility of predicting. If nothing else, Dr. King's murder showed us there was no security in thinking about the future.

For the rest of the day I lost myself in the homework I had neglected since the assassination. I wanted to stay home from school the next day, too, to watch the funeral on T. V. but I knew implicitly that my parents would not agree to this. In their minds, and in mine as well, I guess, I could best fulfill Dr. King's dream by going to school and excelling at my tasks there. At least that's the premise we all cling to, but a hope that now seems less real for my children, surrounded as they are by violence and exploitation.

I left for school the morning of the funeral wearing my usual clothes, those clothes bought for me in Richmond that my parents hoped would suggest that I was like everyone else. But of course, they couldn't buy me a white skin to go along with those pressed chinos, button down plaid shirt, white socks and penny loafers. When I got to school, however, I immediately slipped into the boys' bathroom and took out the strip of black cloth I had purloined from Mother's sewing basket the night before. I fashioned an armband around my left bicep and secured it with two small safety pins brought to school for this purpose.

I received not a few stares when I emerged from the bathroom, and as I joined my friends outside the library, I noticed several of them glancing nervously up and down the halls.

"Are you crazy?" Regina finally asked. "They're never going to let you get away with that."

"I don't care. It's a day of mourning and I want people to

know that I, at least, am grieving. Maybe you all should try it, too."

"You are a fool," Regina hissed. "And a pompous one at that. Don't you think we're grieving, too? Don't you think we're upset? Don't you think I want there to be some recognition of what has been lost? But it's not going to happen and the best thing we can do is go on with our lives, pick up the pieces, and look to the future."

"You pick up the pieces. I want them to lie on the ground awhile. I want people to watch out for them, to look where they are going, to be afraid they might step on them. I want the edges of those broken pieces to be sharp and jagged, to be dangerous." I turned from the group and marched down the hall to my first period class, secure in the knowledge that I was somehow superior. Of course that knowledge was not knowledge at all and I realize now that Regina was at least partially right. Anger gives you an edge, it's true, but there is always a price to pay for such an advantage.

Mr. Estes had scarcely called roll before the office runner arrived with a note from the principal. He'd like to see me, at once, please, and Mr. Estes nodded at me to be excused. I walked down the hall, striding purposefully, passing a few stragglers emerging from the smoke-filled boys' bathroom, ambling off to class. Miss Ayers, Mr. Richards's secretary, motioned me into the principal's office. Sonny Richards was a small, wiry man who had settled in Bluestone after a brief career in minor league baseball. By all accounts, he had been a ferocious and talented player whose dreams of the big leagues were derailed by severely torn ligaments in his right ankle. His injury led him to teaching P. E. and coaching baseball before ascending to the principal's job the same year I started at the high school. Although he no longer coached, he was a fixture at our games, and I knew he respected my skills as a ballplayer. I suspected he also respected my academic abilities, although they likely concerned him less than my prowess on the diamond.

"Sit down, Joe," Mr. Richards said as I entered his office. I lowered myself into the straight-back chair in front of his desk, turning slightly so my left side—and the black cloth on my left arm—was oriented towards him.

Now, I knew Mr. Richards was not the kind of man given to false pleasantries and idle chatter. He understood that being principal meant you were no one's friend: not the teachers, not the parents, and certainly not the students. I respected him for that and for the fact that for three years he had done his best to create in the school an atmosphere of resigned tolerance, if not acceptance. Last year, he had even recommended to the school board the expulsion of a notorious race-baiter who delighted in starting fights whenever possible. Of course the board rejected Mr. Richards's recommendation, arguing that since the boy was a senior, he would be gone soon enough. Publicly rebuffed, Mr. Richards let the matter drop, opting instead to become a conspicuous presence in the young offender's daily routine. He followed him to class, sat with him at lunch, and even shadowed him when he went to the bathroom. His spirit broken, the misguided kid couldn't graduate soon enough.

Now, sitting before him, perhaps I thought Mr. Richards would be sympathetic to my protest. I should have known better as he curtly addressed me, his voice suggesting no possibility of compromise or negotiation.

"Joe," he said, "you need to take that arm band off right now. It is a clear violation of the school dress code and you know it."

In my mind, I quickly weighed my options. If I refused, I would be suspended, and I knew my parents would be disappointed in me. Never mind the principle of the matter. They wouldn't dispute the justification of my convictions, but the bottom line was I'd be punished for a violation of the rules. As my father often reminded me in terms he knew I'd appreciate,

Jackie Robinson suffered great abuse to pave the way for others. I knew his example was the gauge that measured my behavior and the behavior of my friends. I unpinned the strip of cloth and handed it to Mr. Richards, consoling myself with the thought that I had, after all, made my point.

"Thank you, Joe," he said. "Now you head on back to class and I'll see you at this afternoon's game." He dismissed me, and I realized I had not said a word during the conference.

All the way back to class, I continued to rationalize that I had acted appropriately. But deep down, I was disappointed. Maybe Jackie Robinson would have understood, but what about Dr. King? It was his memory I sought to honor, and I felt like I had abandoned him even before his body was in the ground.

I tried to quietly slip back into my seat in the classroom, but I was conscious of quite a few stares. I imagined the smirks of the white students and the surreptitious glances of my black friends. I buried my head in my book the rest of the period, pretending to be absorbed in American History, but subconsciously acknowledging that that history was still being written. I went through that day distracted, unable to focus on my classes and aloof from my friends. All day I felt like I was wading against the current through chest-high water. I kept wondering about Dr. King's funeral, wondering if that advocate of justice and peace, was being, in fact, peacefully laid to rest.

Finally the school day ended, and I trudged to the boys' locker room to get ready for that afternoon's home baseball game. Getting dressed, I felt impervious to the usual pre-game banter and during infield practice I could muster none of the obligatory mindless chatter. Again, I felt isolated from my surroundings, inured from routine concerns of the game. I have some memory of Will uttering some banal remarks in an obvious attempt to draw me out of my funk, but it didn't really register, and he saw the wisdom of leaving me alone.

The top of the first inning passed in routine fashion. Our pitcher, Junior Thomas, was in top form, striking out the leadoff hitter and inducing the next two batters to ground out weakly to the right side of the infield. From my shortstop position, I casually observed the proceedings, thankful I wasn't tested by even the most unassuming grounder or pop-up. As I walked to the batter's box to lead off the home half of the inning, I couldn't shake the lethargy that seemed to envelop me. I think I expected to take three strikes, have a rest, and sulk in my self-inflicted miasma. But I had barely assumed my stance and faced the pitcher before his first offering sailed at my head. Now, I don't think he was really trying to hit me. Strategy-wise it made no sense, and there were enough black kids playing in the district that race-motivated brush backs were no longer routine. No, I just think the poor guy was too juiced up and the ball got away from him. That's why I was surprised when from my prone position; I glimpsed Will charging from the on deck circle towards the mound. Before anyone knew what was happening, he tackled the pitcher and flailed at him with all his night. I leaped up and ran out to pull him off just as both benches emptied. As usual, there was a lot of shoving and posturing, but very few punches actually thrown. Except for Will, of course. By the time the coaches yanked him off that pitcher, that kid was a bloody mess. He had that look that recognizes impending doom and realized that there is no power that can stop it.

When the dust settled, the umpire tossed Will and me out of the game, never mind that I had tried to pull my teammate off his victim. The pitcher was driven to the clinic in town because he looked as if he might need stitches. I know our coach was angry at this display of poor sportsmanship and at the prospect of playing a key game without two of his stars. In the stands, Mr. Richards sat immobile, but it was clear he was fuming. We would be hearing from him, I was sure.

Will and I grabbed our gloves and walked up the hill towards the locker room. Halfway there I stopped and turned to him.

"What the hell was that all about?" I demanded.

He looked me in the eye. "I couldn't let that son of a bitch throw at you," he said as he smiled a big toothy grin. "We're teammates."

Will

You would think I'd be excited about summer—what American teenager isn't?—but when school recessed in early June, I remember experiencing a prevailing sense of foreboding. For one, there would be no summer baseball for me and my high school teammates. We had outgrown little league, and Bluestone wasn't big enough to support an American Legion team. And besides, most of my friends had retreated to their family farms for three months of unstinting labor. Joe would likely be sequestered at St. George's and without the ameliorating presence of high school, our opportunities to interact in socially acceptable ways would be limited. And I was facing the prospect of manual labor at father's store for minimum wage because, as he hollowly said, "it would be good for me."

That spring, The Bluestone Barons had enjoyed a successful season on the diamond, winning the district with a gaudy 17–3 record. Joe, of course, was the star, and he, I, and Junior Thomas were named first team all conference. We thought we had a real shot at the state title—not seen in Bluestone since the glory days of post World War II squads—and we advanced through the first two rounds of the playoffs with little difficulty. But in the regional finals, we met our match in the form of the

Petersburg High School Crimson Wave. These sons of furniture and cigarette factory workers were determined not to lose to a bunch of farm boys, and they received much partisan support in their home ballpark from their fans and umpires, too, or so we believed. Of course, they also had their ace on the mound, fire-balling J. B. Reid, who eventually made it to Double A ball before blowing out his elbow. Reid was an imposing 6' 3" with a sidearm delivery and enough controlled wildness that had us swinging from our heels the whole game.

Those summer days seemed to pass with routine tediousness. I worked from 7:30 a. m. to 4:00 in the afternoon, and my responsibilities chiefly included unloading and stacking bags of seed and feed from tractor trailers driven by middle-aged, corpulent men who took my presence as a signal to stretch their legs and smoke a cigarette. These same bags were later distributed to county farmers in Pointer brand overalls and straw hats in their well-worn Ford pickups. Naturally, these men all knew my father, and as I loaded their orders, I was inevitably asked, "Ain't you Johnny's boy?"

Lunch was from 12:00–12:30 each day, and I usually ate on the loading dock with Willie Whitby, the young mechanic in the equipment shop. Willie was in his mid-twenties, married with two children, and he had been working for my father since he dropped out of high school in tenth grade. Sometimes Champ joined us and I would give him one of the three tomato sandwiches Mother had prepared for me that morning. Champ avowed great affection for "Miz Rawlin's" tomatoes as, with his few teeth, deliberately chewed the tomato, mayonnaise, and Wonder Bread delicacy. Willie's tastes were confined to potted ham or Vienna sausages and an ice-cold bottle of Pepsi with a small bag of Lance's peanuts poured into it as a garnish. We didn't talk much, other than noting the latest exploits of Juan Marichal, Bob Gibson, or Denny McClain in what would become known as "the year of the pitcher" in Major League baseball. More likely, we leaned our backs against cool concrete walls and listened to WLES and DJ Rich Clary on Willie's transistor radio. Just one year older than myself, Rich favored playing the latest Motown hits, but he occasionally slipped in "Mrs. Robinson," "Hey Jude," or the newest release from Herb Alpert and the Tijuana Brass.

After work, I'd meet up with Drew, who was spending the summer as an apprentice butcher at the Red and White, and who, to my way of thinking at least, had thus far miraculously managed to not cut off any of his fingers. Drew always managed to lift a six pack of Schlitz on his way out of work, and we would each gulp a beer on the four-mile drive to the country club. Bluestone Country Club had been created by my grandfather and his cronies from 119 acres of Johnny Walthall's failing dairy farm. Johnny was more than happy to sell the property at a modest loss, lick his wounds, and retire to a double-wide trailer on the shores of Buggs Island Lake, where he could spend his remaining years fishing, raising dogs, and pestering his ever-patient wife, Sadie. The Walthalls' rambling old farm house now served as the club house, and a nine-hole golf course had been carved out of the sloping pasture land.

Drew and I were decent golfers, but neither one of us loved the sport enough to commit to perfecting its many mysteries. I remember that my father took me to Richmond that summer to see an exhibition match at the Country Club of Virginia featuring Jack Nicklaus and home town amateur heroes Vinny Giles and Lanny Wadkins. These golfers provided commentary during their round, and before a given shot, the Golden Bear would explain how he was going to "draw" or "fade" the ball. This was a foreign concept to me who knew only how to swing hard and pray that the resulting shot found the intended fairway or green. Of course, Drew's game was all about brute force. In his mind, there was a direct path from the tee to the green and no topographical obstacle, be it trees, ponds, or sand traps, would divert him from this path. Predictably, his shots were often rebuffed by dense foliage, yawning bunkers, or placid water, and, just as predictably, the offending irons and woods would pay the price for their betrayal. Often I watched in anguished bemusement as Drew, in moments of pure rage and frustration, bent an iron around a Virginia pine or hurled a wedge into a greenside water hazard. His father, an avid golfer himself, refused to replenish Drew's dwindling stock of clubs and by the end of the summer, Drew made his way around the course with a three wood, an eight iron, a four iron, and a putter with a crooked shaft.

Occasionally we would eschew these afternoon matches and drive instead the sixty miles to Richmond and Philip's Continental Lounge. We'd order hamburgers, fries, and Cokes and stare at girls in sundresses, fresh from a day of tanning by the pool of the Country Club of Virginia. We would sometimes buy them a Tab or try to talk to them, but they weren't interested in us, preferring the less obvious (to us) charms of St. Christopher's prep school boys in madras shorts, IZOD alligator shirts, and Sperry Topsiders.

I have to say that the world of girls and dating was still a mystery to me. Sure, I knew plenty of girls from high school, but I never felt I had much in common with them. Or, like Dean, I had known them since childhood, so the thought of actually dating them somehow seemed a betrayal of our friendship. That summer, Drew was dating a girl from South Hill, county seat of neighboring Mecklenburg County. I don't know how he met Brenda, but our golf games often featured vivid commentary on her physical attributes and, according to Drew, her healthy sexual appetites. About the middle of July, Drew announced that Brenda had a friend, Tina, who, at the lovebirds' urging, had agreed to go out with me. Consequently, one stifling hot

Friday evening, Drew and I drove the twenty miles to South Hill where we picked up Brenda before proceeding to Tina's house, a small but trim structure near the railroad tracks. I was relieved to learn that Tina's father, a night watchman for the rail yard, had already left for his job, and her mother, in housedress and curlers, posed no objections or concerns regarding our date.

I have to admit that Tina was very cute: long, strawberry blonde hair, freckles, and a compact figure that had my mind racing at first glance. At Drew's insistence, we drove out to the local airstrip, deserted at this time of night, where we parked on the runway and watched the stars appear above the shadowy pines in the distance. The radio was tuned to a Richmond FM station, but even the sounds of "Born to Be Wild" couldn't muffle the noise from the back seat of the Mustang where Drew and Brenda, I guess, were doing what they normally did. In the front bucket seats, Tina and I made small talk and stared straight ahead through the windshield. At one point, she took hold of my clammy hand and leaned her head against my shoulder, but soon Drew and Brenda were done with their fumblings and we drove back to town for milkshakes from the Dairy Treat. We rode around for awhile, so, I gathered, the girls could be seen with their out-of-town dates. Around 11:00 p. m., we took Tina home. I walked her to the door, and as I leaned in to deliver a chaste good night peck to the cheek, she turned her head and ardently placed her lips against mine. She smiled, ducked into the house, and I was left to chauffer Brenda and Drew and endure their endless questions regarding my thoughts on Tina.

I did like Tina and resolved to see her again, but without the inhibiting influence of my friend and his girlfriend. Consequently, Tina and I soon fell into a routine. Twice a week, I'd motor to South Hill, pick her up, and continue on to the Gaston Drive-In, just over the North Carolina line outside of Roanoke Rapids. There, we would adjourn to the cramped back seat and with the background noise of some "B" movie in our ears, proceed to steam up the car windows. I don't know if I "loved" Tina, but I do know I was drawn to her generous and unassuming nature. I also know our outings were expensive. Remember, I was making $1.60 an hour working for my father, and though gas at Bradford's Esso was just thirty-four cents a gallon, I depleted my weekly pay on the eighty plus miles of driving each date entailed. And let's not forget the cost of the movie, the popcorn, the drinks. I had saved no money by summer's end, and though Tina and I went out a few more times once school began, our romance had fizzled by Christmas.

I don't mean to suggest that I was consumed that summer only by boredom and infatuation. Certainly, I followed the jarring headlines of the day, as reported in the conservative *Richmond Times Dispatch* and by Walter Cronkite on the *CBS Evening News*. Earlier that year, Cronkite had journeyed to Vietnam to chronicle the aftermath of the TET Offensive and, upon his return, essentially declared the war unwinnable. The war was much on my mind that summer, as I would be turning eighteen in a few months and subject to the draft. I had already witnessed a number of graduating friends from high school, friends with no opportunity to attend college enlist in the army and head off to basic training. Would these boys, several of whom had likely never traveled more than 100 miles from Bluestone, soon be fighting in the jungles of southeast Asia? Like my father and brother before me, I knew I would be heading to the University of Virginia after my senior year. I was a good student and my grandmother would help pay my way to Mr. Jefferson's university. Likely, I could avoid, or at least defer military service, despite the long-reaching tentacles of the selective service administration.

That summer, I also followed with morbid curiosity the presidential campaign: the political comeback of Richard Nixon, the June assassination of Robert Kennedy, and the rantings of George Wallace, the candidate of choice among much of the white citizenry of Bluestone. My parents, and many of their friends I suspect, loathed Wallace. While not necessarily enlightened on matters of race, my parents nonetheless realized that times were changing and the world could no longer be mired in the politics of hate. Although I didn't realize it at the time, I think now that I must have been grateful for the insulating presence of my home town in the face of cataclysmic national events.

This sense of security was fissured one evening in late August when my father announced at dinner that Champ's grandson had been killed in Vietnam. William Thomas was the oldest child and only son of Champ's daughter, Minnie, whose husband Champ had banished years ago after Minnie suffered one too many drunken beatings at the hands of this "no account." Champ, himself a widower, had moved in with Minnie and became a father to William and his two younger sisters. According to Daddy, Champ was devastated at William's death, and we would all be attending the funeral that Saturday at the clapboard Mt. Zion Baptist Church out in Meredithville.

I had met William (named after my grandfather, Champ said) a few times over the years at the store. He attended the "colored" high school, where he largely took shop and classes in auto repair. Champ's hope was that one day William, too, would work for my father under Willie Whitby's tutelage repairing International Harvester tractors sold at the equipment shop. Earlier in the summer, Champ had proudly shown us William's official Army photo. With an American flag in the background, William solemnly stared straight ahead in his private's dress uniform. In Champ's words, William would "put an end to that mess over there" and be home soon.

Saturday dawned hot and humid, and after a breakfast of bacon, eggs, grits, and biscuits, we all repaired to our bedrooms to dress for the funeral. My father, my brother Jack, and I put on our dark suits although Daddy sent me back upstairs to polish my wing tips. Mother and sister Cathy attired themselves in their black dresses and, at Mother's insistence, white gloves. We got into the Country Squire and traversed the steamy asphalt roads twelve miles out into the country to the church hard by the railroad tracks. There were a number of cars parked on the packed red clay of the churchyard and even a mule-drawn wagon in the shade of a towering oak by the side of the building.

We walked into the church's dim interior, our eyes slowly adjusting from the day's glaring light. Champ spied us standing uncertainly inside the door and quickly escorted us to the front of the small, but full, chapel. Despite my mother's polite protestations, Champ shooed away from the second pew some unsuspecting family of congregants and motioned us to the now vacant seats directly behind Minnie and the girls. Daddy and Mother quietly spoke to the softly sobbing Minnie and her sniffling daughters. My eyes focused on the flag-draped coffin at the foot of the altar as I considered, probably for the first time, the death of someone roughly my own age.

The service began when Deacon Edwards motioned us to stand as he lined the opening hymn. Suddenly the small edifice echoed with sound, and as familiar as we were with mouthing words from a hymnal, my family soldiered on adding our own voices to the song. I couldn't help but notice how unsteady Minnie seemed during the singing, and when we sat down, her weeping was now audibly pronounced. I remember this service chiefly as a flood of sensations: the chorus of "amen"s during the homily, such a sharp contrast to the mute acquiescence I knew from Emmanuel Episcopal; the constant clacking of beaded bracelets on arms swishing cardboard fans against oppressive heat; the rivulets of perspiration seeping through my white shirts and even my socks; the fidgeting of Jack and Cathy as our bottoms ached from the two-plus hours of sitting in the hard pew.

At the conclusion of the final hymn, six pallbearers, two of whom I recognized as Champ's own sons, carried the coffin out the door followed by Champ, Minnie, and the girls. The rest of us shuffled behind, and I assumed we would head to the car and drive home for iced tea and the Game of the Week with Curt Gowdy and Tony Kubek. Instead, Daddy led us around to the back of the church where a Thompson Funeral Home awning stood over and empty grave surrounded by scattered headstones in a small cemetery. A few folding chairs sat graveside for the family and next to the coffin, to my surprise, two young, white U. S. Army soldiers stood at rigid attention here at what was likely their most foreign posting ever. Despite the heat and buzzing mosquitoes, these young men never flinched as Deacon Edwards intoned the whole "ashes to ashes, dust to dust" liturgy. When he finished, the soldiers somberly lifted the flag from the coffin, crisply folded it thirteen times, and ceremoniously handed it to the still sobbing Minnie.

As the coffin was slowly winched into the grave, I suddenly heard the familiar strains of "Taps" filtering from the woods. The playing was muted, but clear, and it took me and the others a few moments to locate the bugler. He was about fifty yards away in a copse of cedars, standing tall in a dark suit, sunlight dappling off the upraised trumpet. It took me several seconds to sort it out, but when I did, I was surprised, to say the least. The bugler was Joe.

Joe

I first started playing the trumpet in fifth grade, shortly before we moved to Bluestone. Initially, I resisted the whole idea, especially during those first few torturous weeks when I could barely get a recognizable squeak out of the instrument. Still, my father insisted I continue with my lessons; he was hoping, I think, that I might turn into the next King Oliver or Louis Armstrong. My father had always loved jazz. As he liked to point out, it is America's indigenous music, and its development was fueled by talented black composers and performers. He preferred the stylings of these early practitioners of the form, but over the years he developed a love for more avant-garde horn players like Dizzy Gillespie or Miles Davis. Our house was full of albums, and often in the evening, he would put a LP on the stereo console for our edification and my education.

By the time we settled in Bluestone, I had mastered basic scales and a few rudimentary pieces. I continued to take lessons at our new home, and my instructor was Dr. Hicks, St. George's only music professor. St. George's mission was a practical one: educate young Negroes to be useful citizens in what we all hoped was a changing world. The college's curriculum focused heavily on business and commerce offerings, as well as career-oriented paths such as teaching. However, the school (and the Episcopal Diocese which sponsored it) also believed in the value of a good liberal arts education, and thus, people like my father and Dr. Hicks were recruited to fulfill this calling.

Dr. Hicks was a fine teacher, and soon he was coaxing me to practice faithfully and enthusiastically. It seems I was a "natural," and I admit to developing a real passion for playing and discovering just how good I could be. Still, I preferred to largely keep my talent to myself. Sure, the St. George's community knew of my ability as by the time I reached high school, I sometimes played with the college jazz band, although I never understood how five instrumentalists constituted a band. Nonetheless, the group performed a couple of concerts a year for the faculty and student body, as well as a few black business folks from town. Certainly Will and his white friends knew nothing of my trumpet playing. For some reason, I felt it important to have something that I kept close and not share too liberally. I guess I didn't want others to believe that they knew who I was and could, therefore, pigeonhole me to suit their perceptions. Despite the urging of my parents and Regina, I did not join the band at the high school. I didn't want to be part of the Marching Barons, playing worn-out songs and forming a human "B-H-S" on the football field at halftime of home games. Besides, the uniforms were ridiculous, gaudy capes, plumed hats, epaulettes, and lots of braid and brass buttons. No thank you.

It was Dr. Hicks who got me to play "Taps" at William Thomas's funeral. It seems the Army contacted Deacon Edwards in hopes he could locate a bugler, and he, in turn had contacted the college. At first, I didn't want to do it. I didn't know the family at all, and I didn't approve of the war. I guess I arrogantly thought that my participation would lend tacit approval to what I considered to be an unauthorized police action. Fortunately, my mother talked some sense into me as she pointed out that

William Thomas had nothing to do with politics and had died nobly in the service of his country. Besides, as she also told me, I would receive a check for my efforts from the United States government and I could always tear this check up as an act of protest.

I agreed to play and spent a few days practicing. "Taps" is kind of tricky and it took awhile before I learned to hit the high F with confidence. But I did, and that sweltering Saturday morning in late August found me sweating through my suit a respectable distance from William Thomas's grave. When the folded flag was handed to William's mother, Earl Thompson silently cued me and I hit that first somber note. Afterwards, I retreated through the woods where I had left my father's Ford parked on the side of the road and drove home.

That spring, I had followed the Democratic primaries with interest. Like most Americans, I was shocked when President Johnson announced in March that he would not seek re-election, although I didn't for a moment believe he refrained from running to avoid devoting time to "personal partisan causes." No, he had seen the handwriting on the wall; Senator Eugene McCarthy's strong showing in the New Hampshire primary exposed the unpopularity of Johnson's policies in Vietnam. Of course, I liked Senator McCarthy; after all, he had once been a semi-pro baseball player, but I knew he would need more than idealistic college students to actually win the nomination. So when Robert Kennedy entered the race after New Hampshire, I was excited. Now I understand why the McCarthy supporters were so upset; their candidate had challenged an incumbent—who just four years previously had won the office in a historic landslide—and brought him to his knees. But I didn't care. I was drawn to Kennedy's name and family history, his natural charisma, and his empathy for minorities and the poor. And besides, I figured he had the best chance of any Democrat to win the general election given that George Wallace would siphon off traditional Democratic voters in the Deep South.

The night of the California primary found me giddy. It was the last week of school, but I was done with exams and most of my academic obligations. I stayed up late to watch the results, and when the networks called the contest in Kennedy's favor, I felt momentum, and the nomination, was his. I watched the Senator briefly address his supporters (he even acknowledged Dodger pitcher Don Drysdale in his remarks), and leaving the TV on, I went into the kitchen to get a glass of milk before heading off to bed. I was about to turn the set off when my drowsiness was shattered by the announcement, "Senator Kennedy has been shot!" During the chaotic reports from the Ambassador Hotel, I woke my parents with the grim news. They rushed into the living room, and we kept vigil throughout the night. When morning dawned, Kennedy remained in a coma. There was no insistence that I go to school, but I did heed my parents' suggestion that I try to get some sleep.

When I got up a few hours later, I found my mother and father still somberly watching the news. My father had changed out of his pajamas, but he had not bathed or shaved, a rarity for one so fastidious about his appearance. My arrival in the living room signaled my mother into action and she immediately set about preparing a large mid-day meal. We didn't leave the house all afternoon or evening, and just as the rising sun cast its rays through our living room window, Kennedy's press secretary announced that the Senator had died.

What could we say? It had only been two months since Dr. King's assassination, and perhaps we wondered who would be next. I'm sure my mother grieved for his family and especially his mother, who had now violently lost three sons in service to their country. Later, as details of the scheduled funeral began to emerge, we forged our own plan. The Senator's body was to be flown to New York for a Saturday morning mass, and then travel by train to Washington and burial next to his brother at Arlington National Cemetery. My parents decided we would pay homage to the Senator by driving to D. C. for the funeral procession. In the city, we would rendezvous with my mother's first cousin, Lillian, an unmarried career woman who worked at the Treasury Department and who had her own apartment just east of Capitol Hill.

We left our house at 5:00 a. m. for the four-hour drive; Mama had packed cold biscuits and thermoses of coffee for the trip. My father was tense behind the wheel. Cities made him nervous, and the occasion stoked his disquietude. But we arrived at Lillian's without incident and watched the news on her small TV. The flag-draped casket left New York on a private train at 12:30 p. m. for the four-hour rail trip to Washington. Lillian fixed us lunch, and afterwards, we squeezed into her Corvair and drove to her place of work, her boss having ceded to her his parking pass for the day. We wanted a good vantage point to watch the passing of the hearse, and Lillian directed us to Memorial Bridge in the shadow of the Lincoln Memorial. This bridge spanned the Potomac and led to the gates of the sacred cemetery, located on land formerly belonging to Robert E. Lee, commander of southern forces during the Civil War.

A sizeable crowd had begun to gather, but much to my amusement, Lillian elbowed her way through the gathering throng and secured a spot for us right on the curb of the roadway. The first couple of hours passed quickly, but we soon learned from mourners with transistor radios that the train was way behind schedule. We took turns stretching our legs, and the 100 yard walk to the Lincoln Memorial required a half hour of bobbing and weaving through the crowd. I managed to make my way around the edifice and up the stairs to gaze across the Mall, just as Dr. King had five years earlier when he delivered his

"I Have a Dream" speech. What would he make of his dream on this day, I wondered.

I retraced my steps to find Lillian and my parents deep in conversation. It was nearly dusk now, and the train had yet to arrive at Union Station. The adults were debating whether to abandon the vigil and return to Lillian's to watch the proceedings on television. It was my mother who insisted we remain. By nature, she was not a person overtly interested in politics or current events, but something about this occasion touched her to the core. My father wisely acquiesced and we sat in anticipation as the darkness slowly enveloped us.

The train, we learned, arrived at the station shortly after 9:00. News that the motorcade was heading our way led people to spontaneously light candles as beacons for the approaching vehicles. I don't know where the candle I found in my hand came from—maybe Lillian's voluminous purse—but I held it reverentially as the hearse slowly passed by. In that moment, my mother gripped my arm, and when I glanced sideways at her, her own candle illuminated the tears streaming down her face. Afterwards, we silently walked the mile back to Lillian's car and headed to her apartment. We realized how hungry we were and on the way stopped for Chinese take out, a novelty for me, at an all night restaurant on Florida Avenue. Around the small formica table in Lillian's kitchen, we rehashed the day's events and speculated about the future over egg rolls and chicken fried rice. We watched the late news, and were amazed to learn of the arrest that day in a London airport of James Earl Jones, alleged killer of Dr. King. Our stomachs and hearts full, we retired for the evening; my mother shared Lillian's bed while my father bunked down on the living room couch and I on a makeshift pallet on the floor.

I spent that summer working in the library at St. George's, although "working" is probably not the best word to describe how I utilized my time. Sure, I passed a couple of hours each day cataloguing new books and shelving returns. (I can still recall the intricate divisions of the Dewey Decimal System.) I even glued or taped together volumes with broken or worn spines and loose pages. But mostly I read. Usually, I would retreat to one of the big oak tables near the oscillating floor fan and the hours melted in that circulating breeze. Mrs. Reese, the librarian, didn't seem to mind; after all, I really wasn't getting paid much. I think it made her happy just to see me reading. I had no program or course of study; often I grabbed something at random off the shelves and just dove in. I read books of philosophy, works of history and anthropology, "classic" novels, and biography. In this latter category, I gravitated towards works by and about prominent Negroes like W. E. B. DuBois, George Washington Carver, and Booker T. Washington. But certainly, I found nothing in the dusty stacks that stirred me quite like *Soul On Ice*, which I procured when one day I accompanied my mother on a shopping trip to Richmond. While she looked for clothes at Thalheimer's, I perused a couple of book stores on West Broad Street. I was unfamiliar with Eldredge Cleaver or his book, but I still remember the moment in the store when I opened the paperback cover and read the first few paragraphs. I read as much as I could while standing by the rack, but when the proprietor continued to glare at me, I proceeded to the counter and purchased the volume. Of course, I didn't tell my mother what I had bought—I knew she would want to read and upon doing so would not approve—but when we got home I retreated to my room and read the memoir straight through.

I didn't spend all my time sequestered in the library, as my passion for tennis was now in full bloom. Certainly I was inspired by Arthur Ashe who that summer won not only the U. S. Amateur, but the U. S. Open as well, the first black male to do so. Ashe was born and raised in Richmond where he honed his game under the tutelage of his strict father before leaving the segregated city for St. Louis and then California to attend UCLA.

Often, after supper, in the relative cool of the fading daylight, I practiced my own game. There was a backboard at one end of the campus tennis court, and I spent hours rhythmically pounding forehands and backhands just above the net-high horizontal white stripe painted across the backboard. Sometimes, I cajoled Lincoln Thomas, the young, head men's basketball coach to join me in a match. Link was a great athlete and in good shape for someone in his thirties, but he didn't really understand the nuances of the game. He was a defensive player—something his basketball squad was noted for—while I preferred to exploit angles and attack with crosscourt backhand volleys or topspin forehands down the line.

From time to time, I thought about asking Will to play. I knew I could call him up; his parents marginally accepted me, and they had even hosted a year-end banquet for the team at the conclusion of our baseball season. But for whatever reason, I didn't contact Will. I guess I preferred to distance myself from him and the reminders of high school, where, despite my successes, I remained largely unhappy.

Other than books, my one true summer companion was Regina. She and I had a lot in common; after all, we had been in the first small band of Negroes chosen to integrate the schools. And we shared a life as faculty children in the tight-knit community of St. George's. Regina and I hung out together a lot, although we really didn't go out as such. For one, there was no place to go; the movie theater had closed, though whether because of economics or integration was not clear. Secondly, Regina and I had figured out long ago that we weren't "romantic." Still one evening we were taking a walk around campus when we sat down on a bench to talk and watch fireflies. We discussed our thoughts about our impending senior year, plans for college, and the like. I don't know what came over me—maybe I had been reading too many novels, maybe lingering despair over Kennedy's murder, or talk of the future triggered something—but suddenly I leaned over and kissed Regina on the lips. When I pulled away, we stared at each other through the dusk and then we both burst out laughing. Little was said and Regina, to her credit, understood and forgave me for my transgression.

School started the day after Labor Day, and I was enrolled in all honors classes. Will was in four of these classes, and we often walked together from one wing of the building to another. Sometimes, too, we sat at the same lunch table and tried to talk over the din of the cafeteria. We caught each other up on our respective summers, though I did not tell Will about my trip to witness Senator Kennedy's funeral procession. Will asked me about my trumpet playing, but I insisted I was strictly a novice and that "Taps" was part of my very limited repertoire. He delighted in telling me about Tina, and I feigned interest, but I asked him to spare me the intimate details of their relationship.

As the weeks progressed, I found it hard to focus on my school work. Oh, I still did my assignments and made good grades, but I was increasingly disinterested and reticent in class. All seniors were required to take U. S. Government, and in class we dutifully examined the Declaration of Independence, the Constitution, and other documents crafted by the Founding Fathers. To me, these treatises seemed hollow in their promises, as well as their execution. Jefferson's bold statement, "All men are created equal", was countermanded by clauses virtually condoning slavery. And the words of the Constitution's Preamble seemed insincere in a document that declared a black person as only three-fifths of a human being. Given the events of the last six months, I had little faith subscribing to the truth of the tenets proclaimed by "We the People." I was particularly bored in English class; my summer reading had exposed to a world of larger ideas, and I had little interest in scanning the works of England's Lakeside Poets. Only calculus and physics piqued my curiosity. These disciplines were unequivocal in nature and seemed immune to human prejudice.

That fall, Will was particularly interested in baseball's pennant races and the World Series matchup between the Detroit Tigers and St. Louis Cardinals. As a National League partisan, I naturally rooted for the Cardinals and their intimidating ace, Bob Gibson. Will favored the Tigers and their flamboyant 31 game winner, Denny McClain. When the Tigers won game seven behind unlikely hero Mickey Lolich, Will was truly insufferable the next day, and I finally had to pick up my lunch tray and move to Regina's table to escape his gloating. Besides, I was more intrigued in the summer Olympics in Mexico City than the baseball games playing out in the Midwest. And one week after the fall classic's concluding contest, I was amazed to witness 200 meter gold medal winner Tommie Smith and his bronze medal countryman John Carlos raise black gloved fists during the playing of "The Star Spangled Banner" at the medal ceremony. I watched this event with my father who was outraged by the "disrespectful behavior." I didn't agree or disagree with his assessment—knowing it best not to debate my father on matters of disrespect—but I did consider the gesture a brave one.

That fall also found my parents and me considering my college options. Out of a sense of obligation, I suppose, my father asked if I wanted to attend St. George's, but I honestly think he was relieved when I gently declined the opportunity. My parents knew it would be best if I went away for my higher education. Though a southerner herself, my mother determined that I should go north for college. However, she did not want me to go to school on an urban campus, the summer's race riots and burning of cities still fresh in her mind. I spent hours immersed in *The Insiders Guide to College* and other reference works, and I eventually settled on an institution I thought would satisfy everyone's requirements. Hobart College (or, Hobart and William Smith Colleges, officially) was located in the Finger Lakes region in upstate New York, far removed from any major metropolitan area. And like St. George's, it was funded and many years sustained by the Episcopal Church. I liked its emphasis on small classes and its strong academics. And upon examination of the official catalogue, I was pleased to learn that it had a jazz band (more than five member, presumably) and a history of competitive athletics, including tennis (but not baseball). Even Regina approved this choice, noting that Elizabeth Blackwell, the first woman to receive a degree as a Doctor of Medicine, had attended Geneva Medical College, part of the institution that would become Hobart and William Smith Colleges.

Of course, the school was expensive, but my father said the cost should not deter me. There were scholarships available and perhaps some reciprocity agreement for children of college professors. With my parents' encouragement, I applied Early Decision and retreated to waiting for an anticipated response sometime around the New Year.

As Christmas vacation approached, I made a decision, one I agonized over greatly. But once the decision was made, I felt a great sense of relief, and I was at peace with myself. I had been weighing my options for awhile—the pros and cons of not playing baseball for the Barons in the spring—and I finally determined I would, in fact, quit the team. Of course, I didn't want to tell anyone yet because I imagined a whole range of negative reactions, from disbelief to condemnation. Certainly Will would be upset, as would Coach, and I couldn't expect them to understand my reasons. I believed, too, that my parents would be surprised. They, and members of Bluestone's black community, took great pride in my on-field accomplishments. I know that my academic achievement, coupled with my athletic accolades, made me a shining example and a tangible rebuke to the still-lingering prejudices of the town's white citizens.

And what were my reasons? They are hard to explain, even to myself. I think I had tired of team sports. Even after three years, I never felt that I was a totally accepted member of the squad. Certainly there was no animosity expressed towards me, and I was comfortable with Will and a couple of the other players. Yet, I remained the only Negro on the team, unlike the high school's more heavily integrated football and basketball squads. Maybe I figured if I was going to stand out, I preferred to stand out on my own and not as a token presence in a larger group. That's why I decided to direct my energies toward tennis. There was no tennis team at Bluestone High School, so to compete in the sport, I'd have to do so independently. Over Thanksgiving, I wrote the state tennis association and asked for a schedule of spring tournaments. When the list arrived, I saw many events within a three-hour drive, and I began sending in the requisite information and fees. I took a perverse pride in the knowledge that I would likely be competing against white boys who had honed their games on the courts of the Commonwealth's country clubs. But I was eager to test my own game, a game thus far challenged only by Lincoln Thomas and a wooden backboard.

When school recessed for the two-week Christmas vacation, I was excited. I knew I only had one more semester at Bluestone before a new chapter in my life began. But I was also anxious, as tradition dictated that informal baseball workouts began over the holidays. Coaches were not allowed to work with players, but seniors gathered the squad in the high school gym and, using hard rubber balls, led both returning players and would be rookies through a series of throwing drills. Will was eager to assume this responsibility as he likely believed he would be captain come spring. I hadn't yet told him of my plans when he announced on that last day of school that he would see me at 8:00 a. m. on the 28th. I didn't have the heart, or the courage, to say I would not be there.

It was a generally quiet Christmas, distinguished by the usual traditions and rituals. Lillian came to visit, and we enjoyed having her with us, although, as this was her first trip to Bluestone, I'm sure she wondered how her cousin had been exiled to such a god-forsaken place. But the highlight of the holiday was the letter I received on the 27th from Hobart and William Smith Colleges. I was accepted.

Will

It had been a dramatic season, a season where pitching clearly dominated. Just consider some of the statistics: there were 339 shutouts; 82 games ended in scores of 1–0; seven pitchers had ERAs under 2.00. Baseball had never seen anything like it, and I was excited about the World Series and the matchup of pitchers Bob Gibson and Denny McClain. McClain won 31 games for the Tigers, the first 30 game winner in the majors since 1934. How he did it was a mystery to me. It seemed like he spent most of his time playing the organ on television variety shows and flying around the country in his Learjet promoting himself. And to top it off, he somehow also managed to release two albums. Of course, Gibson was equally impressive. His 1.12 ERA was the lowest ever by a big-league hurler with more than 300 innings pitched. So, the Series had the trappings of greatness and seemed a perfect conclusion to the season, a season whose opening had been delayed two days to observe the funeral of Dr. Martin Luther King, Jr. (My father had something to say about that; even World War II had not suspended baseball.)

The first game did not disappoint. The Cardinals won 4 – 0, and Gibson struck out 17 Tiger batters, breaking Sandy Koufax's World Series record, Naturally, I left school early to watch the contest, and my dad came home from work as well. We continued to rendezvous throughout the Series for the weekday games, and we were not the only ones to play hooky. Dean later reported that during the games, the high school was almost as deserted as the first day of deer season. You can bet that my mother didn't approve of my absences, but what could she say while her husband, too, was watching the GE console from the comfort of the living room couch? Gibson and McClain faced each other again in Game 4, and after a one-hour rain delay, Gibson struck out 10 (and even hit a home run) en route to yet another complete game victory. The Cardinals now led 3–1, but the Tigers took Game 5 and McClain won Game 6, 13–1, to set up a deciding Game 7 matchup between Gibson and surprise Tiger star, Mickey Lolich. As a Tiger fan, I was not hopeful, but when Curt Flood misplayed Jim Northrup's seventh inning line drive into a two-run triple, Lolich and the Tigers held on to win the world championship.

I was ecstatic, and I knew Joe would be disappointed. We traded barbs at school throughout the Series, and I understood how much he admired Gibson and his intense competitiveness. What I didn't realize at the time was the diminished importance of baseball in Joe's life. No, his new attitude, if you will, was not apparent to me until he unexpectedly failed to show up for tryouts three days after Christmas. I guess I assumed he'd be there, and I was confused when he failed to appear. Afterwards, I called him, and over the phone he haltingly informed me would not be playing baseball come the spring.

At first, I think I was angry and felt betrayed. I was disappointed because we had a potentially great team with five returning starters from last year's district championship squad with Joe clearly the best player. But mostly, I think his decision confused me. I couldn't understand how someone as talented as he could so easily walk away from a sport he had so obviously mastered. He was, quite simply, the best natural ballplayer I had ever seen, and I have no problem admitting I was in awe of his God-given ability and the intuitive grace that permeated his playing. I had a hard time figuring it out, I really did. He didn't go into the details and the whole tennis obsession did not become apparent until months later. But I did respect Joe because I knew enough of his life at the high school to appreciate that his path had not been easy.

And what about my path? In six short months I would graduate—as state baseball champion I hoped, but now doubted—and then off to the University of Virginia, assuming I finished writing my application essays. But I had no idea what I wanted to study or what I hoped to do with my life. This uncertainty was not unusual I know, but it nonetheless remained a gnawing anxiety in my life.

I experienced that anxiety acutely on Thanksgiving Day. My father had delegated me to take his place in the annual "Turkey Tee Off," a friendly golfing competition designed to get the men of Bluestone out of their respective houses while their wives basted, roasted, baked, and simmered foodstuffs for afternoon feasts. About 25–30 men of the community historically participated in this event, the winner of which received a plaque with a gold painted wishbone affixed to it. Daddy always looked forward to the outing, and he often came home from it perceptibly tipsy, as my mother noted. But this year his own mother had commanded him to help her as she prepared to host the family meal, a novel experience in my memory. To complicate matters, she had invited the Bishop from Richmond and his wife to join us as honored guests. My mother and Cathy were doing much of the cooking, but there was still furniture to move and silver to polish, and my father and Champ had been recruited for this purpose. I volunteered to do the chores, but my mother explained that Granny could not comfortably order me about; she did, however, have a long history of telling my father what to do.

For some reason, Jack was excused from the golf outing. Home from his last year at college, perhaps he received favored-son status and simply declined the opportunity. Therefore, on a cold, blustery morning, I donned sweatshirt and stocking cap and joined the other shivering golfers at the pro shop. I was in the first foursome to tee off, and my partners were Daddy's boon companions: George Turner, Jack Bishop, and Henry Butler. I had known these men my entire life and was as comfortable with them as any teenager can be with someone thirty years his senior. I was mildly surprised to see each man pull a flask from his golf bag and take a nip in preparation to hitting their drives. At their insistence, I went first and with the stares of the congregated golfers fixed upon me, I laced a beautiful drive down the middle of the fairway on the opening 360 yard par 4 hole. My group whistled appreciatively, and then each managed, with varying degrees of success, to propel his ball forward. We hopped into our carts—I was riding with Dr. Butler—and began our odyssey around the brown-hued links.

We played quickly—it was too cold to do otherwise—and I mostly made bogeys with the occasional par. In one transcendent moment, I did birdie the par 3, 184-yard seventh hole. I crushed a four iron off the tee, and the high arcing ball landed on the front fringe before rolling to a stop eight feet from the flag. I was never a good putter, but I steered my ball over the bumpy, dead grass of the green for our foursome's only birdie of the day. My playing partners all had tough rounds; the ball did not travel far in these cold conditions and the constant tilting of respective flasks did little to steady nerves. On the exposed 8th tee, fresh off my triumphant "two," George Turner handed me his silver flask and encouraged me to take a sip. I did so, and managed not to choke or sputter as the amber fluid roweled its way down my throat.

We finished our round and retreated to the clubhouse to warm our fingers and toes and wait for the other golfers to stagger in. George Turner immediately started fixing Bloody Marys, and he casually handed me one as he served the others. I took a sip and looked at the three men seated around the fireplace. George Turner was the county clerk. He had assumed the position many years ago upon the death of his father. As a matter of fact, only during two of the last sixty-one years had a Turner not been the county clerk. That was at the time of the "Great War" when George's grandfather (the first Turner to hold the job) and several other prominent citizens went off to France to be heroes. Sadly (or fortunately, depending on your perspective), the War had ended as the troop transport ship crossed the Atlantic. George was a good county clerk, everyone knew that. Sure, some people didn't like the way he was overly protective of the records, as if he was the sole guardian of a long kept family secret, but, for the most part, they were willing to overlook his fussiness. Earlier in the month, George had just narrowly survived the first contested election of his tenure. His opponent, a young county native just out of college, had considerable support among the area's young people, which were few, and blacks, which were many. Everyone knew George was contemptuous of black people, and he had been genuinely scared that he would lose. He had never been anything other than county clerk, discounting the few years he had unsuccessfully tried his hand at dairy farming. I knew my father was anxious about the election, and he did what he could to help his friend out. It was no secret, apparently, that George was drinking more as he faced the very real prospect of losing.

"Hey Will, do you know what the great white hope is?" I shook my head. "Why, it's sickle cell anemia." The speaker, Jack Bishop, burst into laughter at his pronouncement while I feigned amusement with a smile. I had always considered Jack Bishop, the town's drugstore owner and registered pharmacist, a strange case. He had all the accoutrements of civility, but they somehow failed to camouflage his rough manner. Jack Bishop owned one of the largest, most tastefully decorated houses in Bluestone. His children went to the best boarding school in the state, and he and his wife, Martha, were constantly vacationing at the South's better resorts. Yet Jack Bishop possessed anything but a cosmopolitan air. Quite the opposite, he was coarse and exploitative, having made a fortune overcharging the local citizenry on all their prescription needs. Or so claimed my grandmother, who did not approve of her son's friendship with the druggist.

"How about another drink, Will?" George Turner asked. "We still have a bit of time before the awards ceremony."

"Well, sir, I'm not sure I ought to," I replied.

"Ah, it's all right, Will," proclaimed Dr. Butler. "As your physician, I give you permission. Besides, I reckon that anyone heading off to the University in less than a year should know how to handle his liquor. They did when I went there."

I had always liked Dr. Butler. He had seen me, my brother and sister through cases of mumps and chicken pox, and the three of us each sported scars from football or roller skating wounds that he efficiently stitched up. He could always make us laugh, often at the nature of our own maladies or accidents. He was an unusual man who, according to my mother, had forsworn numerous offers from big city hospitals in favor of remaining in our small town. Today, out on the golf course, I had seen a different side of Dr. Butler. The doctor, who carried a handicap of thirty-one, cursed and violently stomped about whenever he hit a stray shot. At first, I had been offended, but the more I thought about it, his behavior seemed so right. After all, at work the poor man never got a chance to act in anything other than a professional manner. Why shouldn't he blow off a little steam among friends?

"Speaking of the University, any idea what you are going to study?" asked George Turner as he handed me another drink.

"Not really," I replied. "I've always liked history, though. Maybe it's all those Civil War stories Granny told me. I'm just not sure what I'd do with a history degree."

"You could always go to law school," Dr. Butler suggested. "Isn't that Jack's plan?"

"Yes sir, it is. But I don't really think I'm cut out to be a lawyer. Too much work, you know."

"What about teaching?" asked Mr. Bishop. "We could always use a good history teacher at the high school. George and I are on the school board, you know."

"Yes sir, I have thought about teaching." This was true. The idea of teaching was appealing, and certainly it would be nice to have summers free. Maybe even coach baseball, who knows? But not in Bluestone. As this year had proven, teaching in Bluestone was more like refereeing, what with all the racial disturbances in this first year of total integration. No, I'd find a better way to spend my time. I just couldn't get excited about the notion of confiscating switchblades.

"Well, you certainly have plenty of time to think about it," said Dr. Butler, as if he could read my mind.

"Will, you never knew your grandfather did you?" asked George Turner.

"No sir, he died the year before I was born."

"Well, son, I knew him well. As a matter of fact, I always considered him as sort of a second father to me. He was a fine man—always playing ball with your daddy and me, taking us fishing and the like. Anyway, he used to tell me, when I was just a little boy, about what Bluestone was like in the old days. Now your granddaddy came to town in, what was it, 1919, I believe— the year after Mill Hill your family's old place out by the river burned down. According to Billy Buck, Bluestone was so small then that the train from Richmond only came by once a month, and then it backed into town. When your granddaddy came here, he didn't have much to go on, other than his good name and desire to work, and, well, he did all right for himself. As you know, he opened the farm supply store and started raising a family with which I am good friends, I'm proud to say. Yes, Billy Buck did all right for himself here in Bluestone, and I dare say he never regretted a day of his life here. And he wasn't the only one, mind you. There were lots of other folks who forged good lives here. Now, I know Bluestone isn't your booming metropolis full of social life and all, but thanks to people like your grandfather, it's a right nice place to live. I don't mean to preach to you, son, but damn it all, we need to have our children come back to Bluestone. That is if we want the town to grow and keep pace. Now you understand what I'm saying, don't you Will?'

"Yes sir, I understand."

"That's fine. By the way, just how long has the Rawlings family been in the county?"

"Well, according to my mother, since 1737."

"Whew, 1737. Imagine that. I hate to think that the day may come when there are no Rawlings in Bluestone."

"Will," Jack Bishop intoned, "you think about what George just said while you're in Charlottesville, and if there is anything we can do for you or anything you want to talk about, why you just let us know, all right?"

"Yes sir, I sure will. Thank you very much."

"There are plenty of opportunities here, boy," George added. "You just got to be willing to uncover them and do a little work."

All the golfers had finished their rounds, and everyone was gathering for the awards ceremony. I made my excuses—Granny expected us at her house at noon—thanked my playing companions, and headed for my car. I drove the four miles to town with my window down, the cold air lashing away the effects of the two drinks. As I reached the crest of the hill sloping into town, I pulled over and looked at the small community stretched out before me. The bare trees afforded me a panoramic view of the old houses with their expansive lawns.

"God," I thought to myself, "this really is a beautiful place."

1973

Joe

It was a surprisingly cool night in late August, 1969, when we packed the Ford in preparation for the next morning's early departure. I had a restless night of sleep, not from anxiety, really, but more likely, anticipation. I was eager to go off to college, even though I would be attending an institution I had only visited in the pages of its official publications. To me, Hobart represented a departure from everything that was familiar: my family, my friends, my home town, benighted as it was. It was a long way from Bluestone to Geneva, New York, physically as well as emotionally, and I knew that the distance and expense meant I wouldn't be home again until Christmas.

The next morning we set off in the pre-dawn hours, and I felt like a member of Lewis and Clark's Corps of Discovery exploring the unknown continent. We drove all day—Daddy even let me have a turn behind the wheel—and in the late afternoon stopped at a hotel about fifty miles from the campus in preparation for a final assault early the next morning. I took a quick swim in the motel pool and as twilight descended, we repaired to a local diner to eat our last meal as a family for the next three months.

We pulled up to my dorm at 8:00 a. m.—the official start of the move-in period—and quickly unloaded the car. The room was simple: two single beds, two dressers, and two desks. By 9:30 we were done; my mother had even made my bed, and we proceeded to take a self-guided tour of the campus. It was a beautiful day and the lush green grass and stone buildings looked just as I imagined a college should. There was a sense of solidity and promise in the surroundings, such a contrast to the worn, enervated ambience of St. George's. I truly felt I was in a transformative environment, a place that would change me, into what I knew not. Still, I was excited by the prospect.

I knew my father was anxious to leave; his plan was to drive to D.C. and spend the night at Lillian's before returning to Bluestone. My mother choked back tears as we said good-bye, and after uttering the usual platitudes, my father uncharacteristically gave me a hug. I returned to my dorm room to discover my roommate and his parents unpacking his many belongings. Josh and I had exchanged letters earlier in the summer when the college had mailed out room assignments. He was from Long Island, had gone to boarding school, and played lacrosse, a sport I knew nothing about. His parents were prosperous looking and friendly, and his mother gave me a hug when we were introduced. Ian, Josh's twelve year-old brother, kept staring at me in an unsettling way and was strangely quiet when I tried to talk to him. Maybe his parents had not told him that Josh would be rooming with a Negro, but he clearly seemed to regard me with wonder and suspicion.

The magnitude of Josh's stuff amazed me. The surface of his desk was covered with a turntable and amplifier, and three milk crates of albums rested between it and his bed. His open dresser revealed dozens of colorful polo shirts and our shared closet was stuffed with slacks and shoes. Two webbed sticks— for lacrosse, I assumed—leaned in the corner, and the plaster walls above his bed were already adorned with posters of The Doors, The Who, and what would surely have left my mother aghast, Jane Fonda in a skimpy outfit from the film "Barbarella: Queen of the Galaxy." Veterans of dropping Josh off at school, his parents left quickly (but not before his mother invited me for Thanksgiving), and he and I began the process of getting to know one another. We made our way to the dining hall which featured, to my astonishment, a soft-serve ice cream machine. There were not a lot of students eating yet, as the move-in period extended to 3:00 p. m. But I did notice only two or three other brown faces among the diners. Later that evening, our whole dorm assembled for "dos and don'ts" from the Resident Advisor and among the sixty or so assembled boys (or "men" as the R.A. referred to us) there was one other Negro present. We exchanged glances throughout the presentation, and I couldn't help but be reminded of my first year at Robert E. Lee Elementary where I was a painfully conspicuous anomaly in a sea of white students.

That first semester at Hobart remains a blur, but I quickly fell into the rhythm of my new life. The classes—mostly introductory course—were largely interesting and engaging. Surprisingly, my favorite class was Introduction to Cultural Anthropology, a course my advisor suggested when he and I first met to fill out my schedule. This course explored various cultures from around the world and examined human behavior in different societies. It intrigued me, and as a black person in a predominantly white environment, I found the academic language of the discipline oddly resonant.

I quickly learned that if I was going to succeed at Hobart, I would need to work very hard, as Bluestone High School had not entirely prepared me for the academic rigors I confronted. And I did want to succeed because despite the social upheavals of the time, I still believed, as my father always insisted, I could become whatever I wished to be. I quickly developed the habit of spending evenings and weekends in the library. It was not possible to study in my room as on most nights Josh listened to music and drank beer from the endless supply of cans found in the mini-fridge he had somehow procured. I'm not sure how he passed his classes—perhaps boarding school had given him a leg up on college—but pass he did. His goals were modest, as he readily admitted. As long as remained eligible to play lacrosse in the spring, he was happy.

Of course, I did find time to enjoy my new surroundings, a fact I often reiterated to allay my parents' concerns during my ritualistic Sunday night collect calls home. In early October, I sought out the tennis coach who steered me to some upper-class members of the team against whom I could display my skills. On bright fall afternoons, I practiced with a number of talented, affable players donned in crisp white shorts, and I learned to adjust my serve in the teeth of brisk winds off of Seneca Lake. I soon made friends with several of the other black students at the school. There were not many of us, statistically speaking, and certainly I had classes where I was the lone Negro enrolled. We often sat together at dinner to trade bemused stories of our various experiences, and when not in the library, I attended informal gatherings in the common room of one of the freshman dorms. I found much solace in these occasions and embraced the collective spirit they engendered.

And soon enough, I also found myself embracing Melanie Terrell, a first year student from William Smith College, Hobart's separate but equal female partner. Melanie was a light-skinned, slender girl with an imposing Afro; she was passionate about politics and, fortunately, me. Hailing from New York, Melanie actively supported a number of causes on campus and beyond, and her avowed mission was to educate me, who, as she rightly declared, came from "the sticks." (My education wasn't strictly limited to politics as she also initiated my apprenticeship in all things intimate.) The spring of our first year, she helped organize the college's bus trip to New York to celebrate the inaugural

Earth Day festivities at Central Park, where over million people congregated. It was my first trip to Manhattan, and on the bus ride back to school, as Melanie and I held hands, I considered the incongruity of a young, intense black woman from Brooklyn advocating a "return to nature." And though she was just a freshman, Melanie was a vocal presence a month later in the campus response to the shootings at Kent State, shootings that killed four innocent young people.

That spring, I pursued my new interest in anthropology, enrolling in "Race, Class, and Ethnicity" as well as "African Culture," which exposed me to the fact that mankind as we know it had its origins in Africa. I also made the tennis team, but never advanced above the eighth position on the squad's ladder. I did get to play doubles, partnering with a senior, a base-line grinder whose game complimented my own aggressive serve and volley tendencies. And, for the most part, Josh and I got along well; I enjoyed watching his lacrosse games which provided a sanctioned outlet for his vestigial prep-school fury.

By mid May I was done with exams. I put my few belongings into storage, caught a bus to Rochester and a flight to Richmond where my parents picked me up. Melanie had left school a couple of days before me to work as an intern in the office of a New York City prosecutor while Josh had a job as a camp counselor at the same toney camp he had attended as a boy. At the urging of one of my anthropology professors, I had applied for and was accepted to a minority internship program at the Smithsonian Institution where I would receive a small stipend learning the ins and outs of the work at the Museum of Natural History. In addition to enhancing my education and interests, this position offered the added advantage of getting me out of Bluestone for the summer. I was home for a week only, during which my mother tried desperately to fatten me up. I caught up with Regina who had just completed her freshman year at

Hampton Institute where she was studying to be a teacher. Will was also home for another summer of working for his father, and we went out one night driving around the countryside in his Mustang, comparing notes, and drinking beer. (My Earth Day sensibilities were offended when he tossed his empty cans out the window.) There was an ease in our conversation, fueled, I think, by the fact that we had both escaped, albeit briefly, the stifling confines of our small town. Neither one of us knew what our futures involved, but our glimpses of the larger world suggested we might live lives elsewhere.

At the end of the month, Daddy drove me to the Trailways station in Richmond where I took the bus to D. C. I was able to sublet the apartment of one of Lillian's friends who lived in the same building as my cousin. The rent was minimal, but I did have to keep the ficus tree alive, as well as an ornery tabby cat, Archie.

My work at the Museum certainly was not taxing. Mostly, I performed clerical duties and delivered documents to other outposts in the Smithsonian empire. However, I did enjoy meeting the civil service employees and exploring the Institution's vast collections on the National Mall. I was even recruited by a fellow intern to play in a congressional softball league. This intern had a high school friend on the staff of a New Jersey representative who needed a couple of extra bodies to fill out his roster. Games were held on Tuesday and Thursday evenings on swaths of green grass near and around various monuments. While competitive, most contests featured copious amounts of beer drinking by young college students spending their summers keeping the world safe for democracy. Now softball is not baseball, but the basics are the same—hit the ball, catch the ball, and I excelled at both. In my first at bat of the season, I clobbered a home run over the heads of astonished outfielders and staked my team to an early lead. In the field I played shortstop, and I took away many would-be hits with my range and strong arm. As the game progressed, a couple of the opposing players even tried to reach base by bunting, a deliberate flaunting of softball etiquette.

My prowess on the makeshift diamonds of summer softball garnered me much praise and approbation, and even our sponsoring congressman came out to watch one game, his presence a true anomaly, according to his staff. After the games, we often went out for pizza and more beer, and I admit I enjoyed the unfettered camaraderie of these occasions. I also started hanging out with other young interns, exploring various nightspots or attending a play or concert in a park. And on Saturday mornings, Lillian and I often went out to brunch and then played tourist, visiting the capital city's many attractions. I relished these excursions, as I found I could confide in Lillian in ways I could not with my parents. She never judged, just listened patiently and offered soothing suggestions on the subject of my future or my love life.

And speaking of my love life, I did take the train to New York to visit Melanie over the long Fourth of July weekend. I was nervous about this expedition, not because I was seeing Melanie for the first time in six weeks, but because I was meeting her family and I didn't know if I would pass muster. Melanie was shy around me in the presence of her parents, a startling contrast to her normal effusive and affectionate personality. But her mother and father accepted me immediately—Mr. Terrell even declared that I looked like a young Willie Mays—and her nine year-old brother Jamal rarely left my side during the three days of my visit. Everything about Melanie's life intrigued me: her brownstone neighborhood with kids playing in the street, the informal family bantering, the intense political discussions that permeated family meal times. It was a wonderful weekend highlighted by fireworks and a "men's" outing to Shea Stadium where Mr. Terrell. Jamal, and I cheered lustily for the defending

World Champion Miracle Mets. Unfortunately, there was little opportunity for amorous adventures. I slept on the couch in the downstairs TV room, but unlike my parents who unfailingly retired to bed at 10:00 p. m., Mr. and Mrs. Terrell were real night owls. During the nights of my visit, we all stayed up past midnight, so that Melanie and I had aborted and silent make-out sessions after her parents ambled up the stairs. After thirty minutes of alone time the first night, Melanie's mother yelled down the stairs that it was time for Melanie to come to bed.

All too soon, I found myself back at Hobart for my sophomore year, during which I officially declared as an anthropology major. I lived again with Josh and continued to do so throughout my time in college. We had very little in common, and no mutual friends to speak of, but we got along well and tolerated each other's idiosyncrasies. Our relationship was a comfortable one, and I think we both intuitively knew each could depend on the other. I excelled in my classes, which were challenging and stimulating, and I still consider my tenure at Hobart a time of true mental awakening. I made other good friends there, especially among members of the tennis team, where I eventually ascended to the number three singles' player, and the jazz band.

I returned to work at the Museum of Natural History the summers after my sophomore and junior years, and I began to explore possible careers with the Smithsonian. I continued to play softball and even occasionally sat in with my trumpet on amateur nights in jazz clubs in Georgetown. I really enjoyed my summers in Washington, where I had a second mother in Lillian. D. C. is essentially a small town, unlike the discordant metropolis of New York. The capital city was easy to navigate, and it was full of ambitious young people. Many of these young people were black, and I found comfort in the sheer volume of people who looked like me.

During college I spent each Thanksgiving with Josh's family, and even Ian came to accept me as part of the extended clan. Spring Break was always consumed with tennis, and the team usually traveled south to participate in some warm-weather tournament. So my extended visits home were limited to the Christmas holiday. I honestly relished these Christmas vacations. I soaked in the peace of the temporarily deserted campus at St. George's and offered insincere protests to my parents' efforts to spoil me. Strangely enough, I never tired of answering the same questions posed by people like Dr. Hicks or Lincoln Thomas. And, of course, Regina could be counted on for vivid narratives of her own collegiate experiences at Hampton. I spent a lot of time with Will during these holidays when we renewed our ritualistic driving and beer-drinking expeditions. We talked a lot about school, and I could never escape the impression that Will was bored at UVa. He described his life as a series of parties and road trips to nearby women's colleges. He had very little to say about his studies or extracurricular pursuits that didn't involve alcohol and girls. Still, there was an ease between us, and he appeared genuinely interested in hearing about my own experiences.

It was during the Christmas break of our senior year that I came to particularly value Will's companionship. You see, two days before the break, right after my next-to-last exam, Melanie broke up with me. She had been particularly distant ever since we had returned from our respective Thanksgiving vacations, but I chalked up her coolness to the stress of the exam period. We met on that Wednesday night at the Hobart library, ostensibly to study for our final tests. We settled at our usual table in the far corner and I reviewed my sociology notes while Melanie pored over an Econ text. She seemed distracted most of the evening, and as the library was about to close she delivered her fateful pronouncement. In some ways I was not surprised;

with graduation looming a few short months away, we were both aware that our future plans were not entirely compatible. Melanie had already applied to a number of northeastern law schools, and I had been offered a full-time position with the Smithsonian starting the next summer. The past three summers had highlighted the difficulties of a long-distance relationship. Still, the idea of not having Melanie in my life was hard to fathom, and her declaration left me achy and feverish, not unlike the flu that had sent me to Student Health in early November. But I knew the ill effects of losing Melanie were more severe than my bout with the latest strain of antibiotic-resistant illness.

I've often wondered about the timing of Melanie's "We'll always be friends" conversation. We both had a lot riding on our exam performances, and, of course, the holidays were on the horizon. However, in retrospect, the timing of the announcement, like most of Melanie's actions, was well-considered. She knew, I guess, that it was best to break up just when we would be going our separate ways for the month-long hiatus between semesters. I didn't sleep at all that night as I played the conversation over and over in my head. In the morning I reported to my exam, but I have little memory of the questions the test posed or how I answered them. And that afternoon, I caught the bus to Rochester and the plane to Richmond where my smiling parents greeted me. I was pretty morose company, I must admit. At my mother's prodding, I told them the news, and I knew they hurt for me. Of course, there was not much they could do other than offer up hackneyed words of comfort.

On my second night at home, Will called and insisted we get together despite my efforts to postpone our traditional home from college rendezvous. I think he could tell over the phone that something was not right, and, therefore, he would not take no for an answer. He picked me up on that uncharacteristically warm evening, and we decided to drive over to the high school.

Will parked the car, grabbed a brown bag from under the seat, and steered me to the home dugout at the baseball diamond. When he asked, "How's Melanie," I spilled all. He must have known what was up and his prescribed remedy was that I should drink, with his help, the fifth of Jack Daniels he had brought with him.

Now, I had been drunk a couple of times in my life, most notably the previous Spring Break when the tennis team had celebrated a little too intensely after winning a tournament in Charleston, South Carolina. But I was an inexperienced whiskey drinker, and as the night progressed, the clear stars and the full moon did little to illuminate the fog in my brain. Of course, we didn't limit our ruminations to the mysteries of the fairer sex as we traded the bottle back and forth. We talked about the future and the past, our past. Needless to say, I don't remember all the particulars, but I do know I was grateful to Will for his friendship in that moment, and particularly after he somehow got me home and into my bed without waking my parents.

A few days later, Will again came to my rescue. It was early in the morning of January 2. The previous day had been a relaxed one; my father and I watched bowl games together, including undefeated and number one ranked USC's Rose Bowl drubbing of Ohio State behind Sam "Bam" Cunningham's four second half touchdowns. Earlier, we had dined on collard greens, black-eyed peas, and stewed tomatoes, traditional New Year's Day southern fare purported to bring good luck. All was well when I went off to bed, but my mother, distracted and disheveled awakened me at 6:00 a. m. Something was wrong with my father; after a restless night, he was now sweating profusely and reporting tightness in his chest. Dr. Butler was on his way and I best get up. I quickly dressed and went to my father's bedside. Despite his brave face, I could tell he was in pain and worried. When Dr. Butler arrived, he quickly confirmed that daddy had suffered a heart attack, and that he was not out of the woods yet. In the doctor's opinion, Daddy needed to get to a hospital as quickly as possible and the closest and best option was the Medical College of Virginia sixty miles away in Richmond. There was no rescue squad in Bluestone, so Dr. Butler called Williams Funeral Home, and five minutes later Randy Williams pulled into our driveway in his late model, all black hearse. Dr. Butler, Mr. Williams, and I got Daddy onto a stretcher and strapped him into the back of the hearse. Mama and Dr. Butler hopped into the vehicle, and before it sped off Mama instructed me to follow in the family Ford.

As you can imagine, I was pretty shaken up, especially after seeing my father carted away in an automobile traditionally used to transport bodies to their graves. I called Will, waking his parents in the process, and it seemed he arrived at my house the minute I hung up the phone. He could tell I was in no position to drive as he grabbed the keys from my hand and tore off in pursuit of the hearse. We caught up with it just outside of Richmond and Will passed the vehicle so we might arrive first at the hospital and alert the ER. I caught a glimpse of my mother as we raced by the speeding hearse. Her face seemed composed, which I took for a good sign.

The rest of that day was a mixture of anxiety and tedium. When the hearse arrived, Daddy was rushed to the ER, where he was stabilized and prepped for surgery. Two hours later, he was in the operating room where a young cardiologist was performing a cardiopulmonary bypass. Of course, our wait was interminable. Sitting in the hard plastic chairs of the waiting room, my mother and I held hands and uttered comforting, yet hollow words. On more than one occasion, my mother closed her eyes and silently mouthed the words to Psalm 23. Later that afternoon, the surgeon appeared and reported that all had gone well. Daddy was on his way to the recovery room where we would be able to visit him in a couple of hours. Later, he would be admitted to the hospital for what would likely be an extended stay.

Dr. Butler and Will took the surgeon's assurances as their cue to leave. I don't know how they had spent their day; they had not sat with us, respecting, I think, our need to be alone. At one point, Will brought in a couple of White Castle hamburgers, both of which I quickly ate as my mother declined all sustenance. As they were leaving to ride with Randy Williams back to Bluestone, Will handed me the keys to the car and reminded me where it was parked. We thanked them profusely, and veterans as we were at keeping vigil, settled in for a long night.

When we were first allowed to see Daddy, I was shocked. I had never seen him so vulnerable looking excepting, perhaps, the night of Dr. King's murder. He smiled bravely and groggily assured us he would be okay. Later, he was admitted to a room in the hospital's east wing, and to the rhythm of beeping monitors, we took spasmodic naps through the long night in worn, cushioned arm chairs. The next morning, Dr. and Mrs. Lewis and Regina arrived with a small suitcase of Mama's belongings gathered at the house by Mrs. Lewis. After checking on Daddy, we found an inexpensive motel a short bus ride away and checked in my mother. At her insistence, I returned home, Dr. Lewis driving our car through wispy snow while Regina rode with her mother.

Twice in the next six days, I drove to Richmond and back to check on my parents and deliver necessities as instructed by Mama. Daddy was going to be fine, but his rehabilitation would be a long one. The college granted him a semester's leave of absence, and other St. George's professors stepped up to cover his courses. At home, I spent hours robotically cleaning in a vain attempt to exert some control in my suddenly rudderless life. I shopped for healthy food from a list prepared by Mama and filled our freezer with casseroles concocted by the ladies of St. George's. And with Will's help and a twin bed from the college's housing department, I transformed our downstairs dining room to Daddy's convalescent bedroom. On January 10, a full week after his heart attack, Daddy was dismissed from the hospital and allowed to come home. Aware of my fragile cargo, I drove slowly on the interstate, much to the frustration of speeding drivers. Daddy, so glad to be home, protested only mildly about his new sleeping arrangement and began to devote himself to his recovery.

Of course, I didn't want to return to school; I thought it best to stay home and help Mama look after my father. However, Daddy would hear nothing of it, insisting he planned on attending my graduation in May. It was settled, and as Mama pointed out, the people of St. George's were there to help her should she need it. Two days later, Will drove me to the Richmond airport, and full of misgivings, I began my bleak trek back to the cold, snow-covered campus.

Will

All things considered, my graduation from UVa was pretty anti-climatic. My parents came to the ceremony and all, but I couldn't muster much enthusiasm for the event itself. Maybe I was embarrassed or somehow chagrinned because I felt like I hadn't done anything worthy of accolades. I know graduating in and of itself is an accomplishment of sorts, but during my four years in Charlottesville, my grades had been mediocre at best. I did make the Dean's List a couple of semesters, thanks largely to some "gut" classes I was taking and the extensive files of past final exams maintained by my fraternity. Certainly my record did not compare to my brother Jack's who went straight from UVa to law school at Vanderbilt where he won a top prize at his own graduation the week before my own. Jack was staying in Nashville to practice law once he passed the bar exam, and my parents were justifiably proud of him. Although they would never say so, I suspected my folks were disappointed in me and what I considered to be my slovenly college experience. And I'm sure it didn't help that I had neglected to make dinner reservations for the night before graduation when every restaurant in Charlottesville was booked solid. Of course, my mother put on her game face and with groceries bought from the A & P, cooked a meal for the three of us which we ate off paper plates in my dirty, roach-infested basement apartment.

To some extent, I did enjoy my time at the University. My first year, with Jack's urging, I pledged the same fraternity where he was a brother, although I never escaped the feeling that many of the fraternity's rituals were archaic and downright silly. Still, I made many good friends there, and I certainly enjoyed belonging to a place that provided three square meals a day. And, of course, parties at the fraternity deserved their legendary reputation around Grounds. Most Friday and Saturday nights featured two or three kegs, lots of girls, and live bands. And most Sundays involved replacing broken windows, repairing splintered furniture, and mopping beer and vomit-encrusted floors.

I did manage to have a few girlfriends during my years in Charlottesville, although "girlfriends" is probably not the best word to characterize my relationships with the other sex. None of these relationships really lasted beyond a few dates. I think many of my female acquaintances were looking for husband material, and they quickly concluded I did not qualify. But that was fine with me, as many of those first girls who attended UVa when the school went coed my second year, reminded me of the west-end Richmond girls Drew and I used to see at Philip's Continental Lounge in their pink and lime green attire from Papagallos.

As I said, my grades were never anything to brag about. Still, there were courses I enjoyed. I majored in history, and I was drawn to the study of the Civil War and the Reconstruction Era. I'll never forget the History of the South class I took spring semester my first year. My previous experience with history had come from antiquated textbooks at Bluestone High and the highly embellished stories told by my grandmother. It never occurred to me that "facts" were open to interpretation, and I remember the confusion and excitement I felt as I read disparate, conflicting accounts of the time by different academics. If nothing else, I came away from that class with a redefined sense of slavery, the "peculiar institution."

Graduation itself was a desultory affair. It was a gray, misty day and the commencement address by a UVa alum and cabinet secretary was less than inspiring. In my rayon gown and cardboard cap, I processed and sat with my fraternity brothers, many of whom were visibly hung over. After the ceremony, my parents and I retreated to my apartment where my father and I quickly loaded the pickup he had borrowed from the family store. Mother gathered my clothes and packed them in the trunk of my car and by three o'clock we were on the road to Bluestone, Mother riding with me while Daddy drove the truck.

It was strange to be living at home again. I certainly never expected to do so, and you can bet my parents didn't expect it either. But there I was, ensconced in my childhood bedroom with model airplanes on the book shelf and a poster of Mickey Mantle on the wall. My plans for the future were fuzzy, to say the least, and I quickly fell into my old habits and routines. I started working again at the loading dock (with a raise, slightly above minimum wage) where I endured good-natured ribbing from Champ and Willie about how "soft" I had become. Drew and I resumed our after-work golf outings, though as head butcher at the Red and White, he no longer purloined our beer, mindful of the threat to job security such an act represented.

I occasionally saw Joe, who was home for a few weeks before starting his job in D. C. We'd sometimes ride around, have a beer, and talk about the future. But, in truth, these excursions were dispiriting for me as Joe's vision of his future was much clearer than my own muddled view of the road ahead. From time to time, he also convinced me to play tennis with him. We'd meet on the court at St. George's where Joe mercilessly proved just how out of shape I'd become. Still, I did what I could to help him keep his game sharp, as I knew he hoped to play in some amateur tournaments later that summer in Washington.

But clearly the highlight of my return home was my discovery of The Red Fox Tavern, a combination beer joint and lunchroom newly opened out by the man-made, hydroelectric generating lake south of town. Often, I'd drive out to the Red Fox after work for a hamburger and a cold beer, and it wasn't long before I struck up a playful acquaintance with Sara, one of the waitresses. A year or two younger than I, Sara and her parents had recently moved to the area from Louisiana, her father hired as a timber marker for one of the large pulp wood companies in the county. Sara was a beautiful girl—truly—with long, sandy brown hair and big blue eyes. And she was funny. You could tell she didn't take herself too seriously, and she was pretty comfortable poking fun at "college boy" as she called me. There was a real ease about Sara, and I was comfortable talking with her. About the only thing I didn't like about Sara was the fact that she incessantly chewed gum. I don't mean that she discreetly worked over the Juicy Fruit; no it was more of an audible smack, smack, smack. I don't know why I found this habit so offensive, but I did. You'd think my years with tobacco and Bazooka chewing baseball players would make me somehow immune to this tendency, but it didn't. Maybe it just seemed so incongruous that such a pretty girl had, what seemed to me, such an indelicate habit. But no matter. Soon I asked Sara out on a real date, and in the dark of the movie theater in Roanoke Rapids, her gum chewing seemed more noticeable than ever. As I drove home after the movie, I finally screwed up my courage and told her that her gum chewing really bugged me. Thankfully, she wasn't offended, but she did point out that she was not fond of the fact that I bit my fingernails, a habit that my mother had despaired of breaking in me for many years. Sara and I both laughed, promised to reform, and when I pulled off on a secluded cul-de-sac near her house, we exchanged memorable kisses (after she had tossed her gum out of the window).

Before you knew it, Sara and I were an "item," and we introduced each other to our respective parents. No one raised objections to our courtship, at least not to us, not that it would have mattered if they had. I don't mind admitting I was smitten by Sara, and by the Fourth of July we were spending as much time together as we could. She was a constant revelation to me. At first, I think I arrogantly assumed that Sara must not be real bright, given the fact that she had not gone to college. Fortunately, I realized just how ignorant in fact I was. Sara was one of the smartest people I had ever met; she just didn't like school, that's all. She was incredibly well-read and consumed many of those "classics" that intimidated me. Increasingly, as I got to know Sara, I could imagine a future that involved her as part of my life.

Despite, or perhaps because of Sara, by August I had determined that I needed to get out of Bluestone. I knew I could not work forever for my father, even though that is essentially what he had done upon his own graduation from college. But that was different. My grandfather was sick by that time, and he needed Daddy to run the business and provide for the extended family. I began thinking about law school encouraged, perhaps by Jack's example. (Though I knew with my undergraduate record I could not aspire to attend a top notch school like Vanderbilt.) And, as my mother was fond of pointing out, her father had been a "barrister" in her small South Carolina coastal town. By mid-August, I had a plan. Daddy had spoken to his brother-in-law Gilbert, husband of my Aunt Margaret, and he offered me a job with his small highway equipment company in Richmond. Better yet, I could live in a cottage on Gilbert and Margaret's property, a woodsy twenty acres on the banks of the

James River, just a thirty-minute drive from the heart of the former capital of the Confederacy. The cottage had once served as the office of Gilbert's home-grown business, and it contained a small kitchenette, in addition to the bath and two other rooms. (I think the former office must have also served as Gilbert's retreat or refuge because as everyone in our family speculated, life with the volatile Margaret could not be easy.) Anyway, the childless couple welcomed me to my new digs over Labor Day, and I began preparing for my new life, a life I imagined would feature fulfilling work during the day and studying for the LSAT in the evening.

Uncle Gilbert's business was a unique one, or so it seemed to me. Basically, he bought used highway equipment from the Commonwealth and other states, reconditioned it, and sold it to private contractors throughout the Old Dominion and beyond. My apprenticeship was a short one. I spent a couple of weeks traversing the state with Gilbert, visiting road projects massive and small, and assessing equipment needs from job foremen. These fact-finding missions, as Gilbert called them, led to unannounced visits to far-flung company headquarters where my uncle tried to jovially convince executives in work boots that they needed to upgrade their machinery. He was often successful with these entreaties, and he soon launched me to carry out this work on my own. Most of my forays were day trips, begun before dawn to Hampton Roads or the Shenandoah Valley, surgical strikes that reminded me of the movements of Stonewall Jackson's troops during the Civil War. Sometimes I was gone for two or three days on visits to Southwest Virginia and the alien culture of the coalfields where roads were in need of constant repair from overburdened coal trucks. These trips often found me bivouacked in some small motel by the highway in Big Stone Gap, Grundy, or Norton. On these nights, after a "country style" meal in a local diner, I'd retire to my room with my LSAT study guide and a pint of Jack Daniels, often falling asleep to the rumble of heavy-laden Norfolk and Western coal trains en route to the state's port cities. Most evenings, however, were spent at the cottage where I'd grill a hamburger topped with the season's last tomatoes from Uncle Gilbert's expansive garden. I loved those solitary evenings and the clear chorus of crickets and bull frogs that serenaded me from the surrounding woods.

Some nights, I'd reconnect with a fraternity brother or two, Richmond boys returned home to assume the mantle in some family-owned business. We'd go out drinking in Shockhoe Bottom, or occasionally spruce up to dine at the Commonwealth Club with my friends' parents. That fall, I went to two or three weddings of college friends, grand affairs with lavish receptions at the Country Club of Virginia. These events featured open bars with good bourbon and single malt scotch, slabs of roast beef thinly carved by white-aproned black men with starched hats, and bowls and bowls of glistening fresh shrimp. I'd dance with erstwhile "girlfriends" or other pearl-bedecked girls from college who shimmied to beach tunes and soul classics as played by one of the party bands of the era.

Once or twice a week, I'd call Sara, and in her sweetly modulated voice, she'd recount the latest happenings in and around Bluestone and peevishly ask me if I missed her. And of course I did. Soon Sara started visiting me every other weekend, arriving late on Friday evenings after driving two hours at the conclusion of her shift at the Red Fox. Naturally, I had asked Uncle Gilbert and Aunt Margaret if it was okay for Sara to visit, expecting them to insist that she stay in the guest room in their house. But to my delighted surprise, no such insistence materialized as they seemed to take a perverse pride in our "illicit" rendezvous. Besides, they loved Sara immediately. Raised in the mountains of Virginia, Uncle Gilbert was a country boy at heart, and he embraced Sara's unpretentious demeanor and good manners. And Aunt Margaret was drawn to her from the start, treating her like the daughter she'd never had, a daughter with whom she bypassed the angst of adolescence and the rebelliousness of the teenage years. A daughter who, instead, arrived on her doorstep a full-blown young woman with an open heart. And Sara seemed to bask in the love she felt from my aunt and uncle.

On the Saturdays of her visits, Sara and Aunt Margaret went shopping downtown while Uncle Gilbert and I rose early to go turkey hunting or tailgate at home football games of the University of Richmond Spiders, Gilbert's alma mater. We'd gather again in the evenings for dinner, Sara often in a new stylish dress from Miller and Rhoads or Montaldo's. Uncle Gilbert grilled steaks and opened a bottle of good wine, and we enjoyed a leisurely meal lasting far into the night. Of course, I reveled in these moments of domesticity, and I spent long minutes gazing at Sara. On Sunday mornings, she and I drank coffee and read the paper in bed, just like a married couple, I thought. But too soon, Sara would leave for her afternoon shift at the Red Fox, serving sandwiches and cokes to sunburned families fresh from a day of boating on the lake, and I would return to my LSAT review.

All in all, it was a glorious fall. I enjoyed my job with Uncle Gilbert, and I particularly relished my trips to the nooks and crannies of the state, many of which I had never visited before. The small towns and cities I found there were sources of endless fascination, poised as they seemed to be between the tension of the past and the promise of the future. And I looked at them with a discerning eye, fantasizing which might be a place to settle down and raise a family. Increasingly, I thought, Bluestone was not such a place, despite my long-time family connection to it. Contrary to the claims of George Turner and Jack Bishop, there was in fact, little opportunity in the home of my progenitors, and Charlottesville and Richmond, in varying ways, had exposed to me a world of possibility. And besides, no matter what I did with my life, I would always be Anne and John Rawlings's boy.

And believe it or not, I enjoyed that fall's self-prescribed program of study. I was attracted by the LSAT's exercises in logic, and it was good to engage my mind when it was not in a constant beer-infused haze. I responded to the satisfaction of setting and meeting study goals as self-discipline had never been my strength in college, and I found myself in mid-November cloistered in an airless room at the University of Richmond taking a test that would likely determine my future.

And Sara? The more I thought about her, the more determined I was that she should be my wife. True, we had known each other only a few months, but those months had been the happiest of my life. Besides, hadn't my own parents gotten engaged on their second date? Of course, that date was the same day Pearl Harbor was bombed and the certainty of the future was dramatically called into question. When Sara visited me the weekend before Thanksgiving, I proposed to her while we walked along the banks of the river. The night before I had confided in Aunt Margaret, who was genuinely pleased by my intentions. But she was shocked to discover I had no ring, and she quickly retrieved and bestowed upon me a ruby and diamond band she had inherited from my great-grandmother. When Sara said "yes," it was a truly cinematic moment, and I was convinced that this was one movie where everyone would live happily ever after. Uncle Gilbert and Aunt Margaret insisted we all go to the Commonwealth Club for a celebratory dinner, and I know it galled them that they couldn't share our good news with friends they encountered there. I had asked for their restraint until our respective parents were informed, and Sara, as a concession, wore her new ring on a chain around her neck.

In my mind, the wait would be a short one as I planned to announce our good news the following week at Thanksgiving. On that day, I was invited to a mid-day meal at Sara's family home out by the lake, and she would join my family at our evening feast. I really liked Sara's parents, who were as unassuming and self-deprecating as their daughter. And although they didn't know me well, I sensed they were fond of me, especially Mr. Johnson who seemed to enjoy having another man around the house. At halftime of the Cowboys-Dolphins game, we went outside to toss the football. Under the towering pines that lined his driveway, I told him Sara had agreed to marry me, and I asked for his blessing. He hesitated—just to make me sweat a bit, I think—before slapping my back, grasping my hand, and replying in the affirmative. Back inside, he shared the news with his wife who literally squealed in response. They admired the ring which Sara revealed, and the next hour over dinner was consumed by questions and particulars, many of which we could not address. Soon, it was time for Sara and me to drive the fifteen miles into town for the Rawlings family meal.

Thanksgiving in my house was always a production. After we "freshened up," Sara and I joined the clan in the living room for cocktails. Sara was not really a drinker, but she did accept a glass of sherry from my father, still a bit glassy-eyed from that morning's Turkey Tee Off. He poured me a bourbon and water, and we settled in for the usual small talk and awaited the summons to the table from Mother, laboring in the kitchen with Ruth, now in her twentieth year as the family maid. (Sara had not known what to make of Ruth when they first met; her only previous encounters with maids had been in the novels she read.)

Granny was there, of course, resplendent in a royal purple dress, and Jack and Cathy were both home, from Nashville and Virginia Beach, respectively. Everyone was dressed up—family tradition dictated that the men wore jackets and ties to the meal—and I could tell Sara was a bit anxious at this prolonged exposure to my extended family. I was about to fix a second drink when Mother beckoned us to the dining room where the table was set with her best linens, china, silver, and crystal. Daddy intoned his usual blessing, and as we all sat down Daddy began serving the turkey which Mother had already carved in the kitchen. Sara was seated across from me, and we exchanged smiles during the passing of assorted bowls of heaped vegetables, gravy boats, and dishes with cranberry sauce and pickles. As usual, it was a scrumptious meal enlivened by Granny's commentary, as she always maintained one of a lady's chief responsibilities was to be a pleasant dining companion. She graciously engaged Sara in the conversation and delighted in her stories of some of the more colorful patrons at the Red Fox Tavern.

As Ruth cleared the dishes in preparation of dessert, I stood up and walked around the table to stand behind Sara's chair. I proclaimed that I had an announcement to make, and I did so. There was a moment of anxious silence before the clapping and congratulations ensued. Daddy ran to the kitchen to fetch a bottle of champagne, kept in reserve for visits by the Bishop, and, after filling everyone's glass, proposed a toast to the happy couple. Everyone hugged Sara, and as we ate sweet potato, pumpkin, and pecan pies, Mother was already planning the wedding. There would be a rehearsal dinner at the country club for the families and the wedding party, and she hoped Sara's parents wouldn't object to having the ceremony at Emmanuel. Granny offered to host the reception at her home, and I knew that within a few days, Mother would invite the Johnsons to lunch so they could meet and begin discussing details.

I expected Sara to be overwhelmed by all this fuss, but she basked in the attention. After supper, she and I put on overcoats and went to sit in the rocking chairs on the front porch. We held hands, and watched the occasional car pass by as we talked about our future, a future full of uncertainties, but one we would face together.

Joe

Graduation day dawned bright and clear. The trees were in full bud, the green lawns of the campus grounds were lush and crisp, and a mosaic of colorful flowers were starting to bloom along sidewalk borders. And on this gloriously crisp day, my last at Hobart, it was easy to remember those things that had initially attracted me to the school. Of course, Mama and Daddy had made the trek northward for the occasion, and it was the first time I had seen my father since I returned to school ten days after his January heart attack. He had lost weight and his hair seemed decidedly more gray than I remembered it. He walked deliberately, but his carriage was erect, and we embraced one another at first encounter that graduation morning. I was happy to see him and his presence seemed to dispel the many doubts and anxieties I had harbored the last few months. And I was glad that I would have a month at home with him and my mother before starting my job at the Smithsonian.

I knew my parents were proud of me, but I was proud of them as well. Despite the societal obstacles of their day, they had forged a good life together, and I couldn't stop beaming at their presence. Of course, my father had on his best dark suit, a sharp contrast to the casual seersucker jackets or blue blazers worn by most men in attendance. And ten years after the golden era of Camelot ended with President Kennedy's assassination, my mother wore her white pillbox hat, much like the ones favored by the former first lady. I delighted in introducing them to my friends and my professors, all of whom were surprised when my parents thanked them for the ways they had helped me the last four years.

The ceremony itself featured the usual clichéd remarks, as one speaker after another reminded us of our good fortune and encouraged us not to squander the opportunities that had been granted to us. All too soon, however, it was time to pack the car, and I repeatedly reminded my father he was not to lift anything heavy. I said good-bye to Josh, who would soon begin work at his father's investment firm, and I knew that probably nothing in his life would match the euphoria he felt the previous spring when the Hobart lacrosse team had won the national championship.

I spent most of the trip home telling my parents about various friends I had made and their ambitious plans for the future. I was excited about my own plans as well. After three summers in Washington, the capital city really did feel like home. I loved being connected—although, admittedly, very tangentially—to the "halls of power." And I also loved the cultural vibrancy of the many artistic and historic attractions, not the least of which was the venerable Smithsonian, my once and future employer. Of course, I was cognizant of the fact that everything in life was subject to change, but still I had no trouble imagining a career spent in service to the Institution.

Once home, I was happy to see the dining room restored to its intended purpose as all traces of Daddy's convalescent bedroom had disappeared, Still, there were concessions to his new "lifestyle," chief among them his diet. Gone largely were the previous staples of red meat and fried food, replaced by broiled fish and chicken and fresh vegetables. And I was surprised to discover a small garden planted and maintained by my mother (never known for her green thumb) mere steps from the back door. Exercise was also part of Daddy's new regimen, and he rose early each morning to walk laps on the track that circled St. George's football field. Often, I accompanied him on these walks, and we talked about the latest revelations of the Watergate Committee, whose hearings were being exhaustively covered by the national networks.

I have to say I was as happy that month as I had any right to expect to be. I was a college graduate with the promise of a good job, and the people I loved and who loved me were healthy. I think I had even emerged from the suffocating miasma of my breakup with Melanie. I thought of her little these days, and in those moments when memories of her did leak into my consciousness, I somehow managed to will them away. And of course I was excited to be an usher at Regina's mid-June wedding at St. George's. A scant month after their graduation, Regina and her college sweetheart Steven Bowser exchanged vows at the St. George's chapel before setting up house in Norfolk, where they both had jobs in the public school system. Regina was my oldest friend, and I was buoyed by her happiness and obvious devotion to the strangely intense, but humble, Steven.

And I did see Will, who I coerced into playing tennis with me, and with whom I shared a beer or two on humid nighttime drives about the county. He was working for his father, but had recently decided to take the LSAT and apply to law schools. He was also in the first throes of his infatuation with Sara, and I was glad he seemed committed to something besides getting drunk. But I was hesitant when he insisted I meet her. To some extent, I think, Will had moved beyond regarding me as his black friend, and to his credit he considered me his friend, period. And certainly I considered him as such, as his actions last Christmas had demonstrated. Still, I was ever conscious of our different races and all the difficulties that difference implied. For example, despite their overt hospitality, I never escaped the feeling that Will's parents would have preferred their son not be friends with a "colored" boy. During rare visits to their home, I noticed their sidelong glances and forced smiles. In general, I was used to white people acting overly earnest upon meeting me, as if they were consciously tamping down long-held prejudices and misgivings. I didn't want to meet Sara and see her face register that false assuredness. I didn't want Will to be somehow disappointed in her or, perhaps, me.

But I shouldn't have worried. I had convinced Will it would be best if I met Sara in circumstances other than having a meal at the Red Fox. There, I reasoned to myself, she was paid to be nice to strangers. Still, I agreed to ride with him early one Sunday evening and pick her up from work. She would bring a picnic dinner with leftovers from the restaurant and Will, of course, would provide the beer. She was waiting outside for us when we drove up and I got out of the car in order to be introduced. Before Will could dispense with the formalities, Sara walked right up to me and gave me a big hug. Initially, I was taken aback—raised as I was in a family not naturally demonstrative in its affections— but I was moved by her genuine embrace. She was, she said, delighted to meet Will's best friend. She insisted that I sit up front with Will on our drive to a shady grove on a quiet inlet of the lake. Will didn't talk much during our meal, deferring to Sara and her apparently limitless questions. But I didn't mind, as these questions were honest and unassuming, like Sara herself. I understood why Will liked her and I told him so, not that he needed my approval, after we had taken her home.

As one who had majored in anthropology, I was naturally curious about human origins, and that summer I was interested in learning more about the beginnings of my own family. I knew that my great-grandfather had grown up out in the county on the old Rawlings's plantation, and that for some reason he had been granted forty acres of that land by the Rawlings family. Was it because of his loyalty and hard work, or, as my father had intimated, his blood connection to Will's great-grandfather? My father knew little of the family history before his grandfather Joe's own existence. And indeed, it was perhaps not possible to know more than the relative certainty that Joe's own parents had once been slaves. Still, I wanted to learn more, not for any perverse satisfaction, but, rather, to simply better understand myself and this place, a place I would soon be leaving and likely never living in again.

I spent a couple of days at the courthouse, looking at old wills and deeds in the Clerk's office. Now of course, that information is all public, but it's fair to say that George Turner seemed suspicious of my motives. Oh, he was polite and all— asking how he could help me and the like—but he appeared to make a careful mental note each time I pulled out another volume for review. And when he went out to lunch, the county administrator's secretary managed to find herself in the room engaged in her own research.

I did find the deed that transferred the parcel of Rawlings's property to my great-grandfather. But, not surprisingly I guess, this "gift" did have strings attached. The document stipulated that my great-grandfather Joe pay the Rawlings family twenty percent of his farm's earnings each year for twenty years. At the conclusion of the prescribed arrangement, the acreage would belong to Joe, free and clear. However, if he missed one year's payment, ownership of the farm would revert to Paul Rawlings. While not technically sharecropping, the conditions of the deed virtually assured a degree of financial servitude. Of course, I wasn't sure if such an arrangement was even legal, but my great-grandfather must have fulfilled the obligations of the contract and owned the land outright by the time my father was a boy.

And when Joe died, my grandfather in Detroit sold the property for a modest amount, likely assuming that the Washington family connection to Bluestone had been permanently severed.

I also looked in the books that held all the old wills to see if I could find any mention of my great-grandfather in the final bequests of the Rawlings family. Edward Rawlings's testament was interesting. Dated 13 September, 1846, the second paragraph of the will made the following provision:

"To granddaughter Nancy Rawlings, the daughter of my son Paul Rawlings, Little Fanny, child of my Negro woman Amy."

I was troubled by the preposition "my" and all it implied. Of course, Amy was a slave, and much of Edward Rawlings's will detailed what was to become of his vast holdings of slaves upon his death. But I wondered about Amy. Could his "Negro woman" also be his concubine? Could Little Fanny have grown up to be Joe's mother? That could explain, perhaps, why Paul Rawlings ultimately ceded land to my great-grandfather. Of course, there was no way of knowing for sure, at least not from the courthouse records here in Bluestone, and I knew further research would have to wait.

I moved to Washington over the Fourth of July weekend, my job scheduled to begin the following week. The ever-resourceful Lillian had again found me a place to live, a small one bedroom apartment on the top floor of a rowhouse near Capitol Hill. There was a bus stop just outside the building, and I even envisioned fixing up my old bicycle and riding to work on nice days. Lincoln Thomas helped me with the move. Somehow, Daddy had convinced the college to loan us the small panel truck that ferried supplies to and from the dining hall, and Lincoln and I loaded it up with a few remnants of my dorm-dwelling days, as well as some secondhand pieces of furniture, including a bed and a sofa, acquired at the Eternal Attic, Bluestone's thrift shop. I had not seen the apartment, but Lillian had sent me her hand-drawn floor plan and a detailed list of the furnishings she believed the space required.

My parents didn't accompany Lincoln and me on the trip. My father still had to guard against over exertion, and I knew my mother was disappointed not to be able to offer the maternal perspective regarding the placement of the furnishings. They planned to visit later that summer, and I promised Mama I would not do too much "decorating" until she arrived. The drive was long and hot as we plodded north along Interstate 95, congested with holiday traffic. Lincoln set off a cacophony of blaring horns and squealing tires as the lumbering truck merged onto the 14th St. Bridge. We dodged the ubiquitous Metro construction and showed up an hour late for our appointed rendezvous with Lillian, who had obtained the key from the landlord. After a quick inspection of my new home, Lincoln and I started wrestling my furniture up two airless flights of stairs, and I speculated that this day would likely mark the end of my friendship with Lincoln. Much of the furniture had acquired a stale produce smell during the four plus hour drive, and Lillian opened the sliding balcony door to welcome the less oppressive smells of the city. We were done unloading around 2:00 p. m. and I offered to take Lincoln and Lillian to lunch. But they demurred. Lincoln was eager to get back over the river and on his native soil and Lillian was already late for a picnic with co-workers at Hains Point. Making sure the key was in my pocket, I set off to explore my new neighborhood before assembling my bed and tacking the boxes strewn about the open kitchen, dining, and living room space.

Within a few days, I felt like a native Washingtonian. My previous tenures in the capital city had been finite, confined by the boundaries of summer jobs. Now, however, the limitless future stretched before me, and I took a proprietary interest in my new home town. I quickly discovered the neighborhood grocery, the best pizza place, and the closest tennis courts. I was excited about work, and I showed up forty-five minutes early on my first day, sporting a new blazer Lillian had bought for me the day before at Lord & Taylor. My new position at the Museum of Natural History was an administrative one, but that first month on the job—at the direction of my supervisor—I acclimated myself to all facets of museum employment. I helped set up new exhibits, sometimes working with taxidermists, and I researched and wrote accompanying information panels. I enjoyed the camaraderie of the staff, and like a veteran employee, I, too, soon learned to complain about the unfathomable antics of the museum-going public.

Outside of work, I reconnected with my old softball team who welcomed me back as if I was Hank Aaron. Of course, many of the regulars from summers past had moved on, but there was still a core group of players from the congressman's full-time staff. A few new faces—summer interns, friends of friends— filled out the roster. Among these faces was one that immediately attracted me, and I soon found myself talking with Aisha Evans, who hailed from our sponsoring congressman's home district in New Jersey. Aisha had recently graduated from Spellman and was commencing a graduate program in African Studies at Howard University. Her parents were supporters of the congressman and the previous year he had written a recommendation on her behalf for a state department summer internship in Kenya. Upon moving to D. C., one of the first things Aisha had done was to stop by and thank the congressman at his office where members of his eager staff recruited her to the softball team.

I learned most of this information the evening of my first game back. The team elders immediately installed me at shortstop, my old position, replacing a petulant summer intern from Rutgers. Aisha played second base, and while her throws to first were often erratic, it was clear she was a graceful athlete.

We chatted between innings, and when the team went out for the obligatory post-game pizza and beer, I made sure I slid into the crowded booth next to Aisha. Later, as we departed the restaurant, I asked Aisha for her phone number which I wrote on a paper napkin at the counter.

In the weeks that followed, I saw Aisha as much as our schedules allowed. I took it upon myself to be her tour guide, and I escorted her to my favorite attractions in and around the city. We had much in common, including, obviously, our interest in Africa, although our migration to Washington had followed opposite paths. I, a southerner, had gone north to college, while she, born and bred in the Garden State, had traveled south for her education. When my parents came to visit in late August so my mother could, as she put it, "freshen up" my apartment, I introduced them to Aisha. They hit it off right away, and during the dinner Mama insisted on fixing, I could scarcely get a word in. Of course my father, the professor, took a keen interest in Aisha's course of study, and both of my parents were intrigued to learn of her summer sojourn in Africa. By the end of the evening it was clear that they "approved" of Aisha, and she in turn expressed her admiration of them as I drove her back to her apartment in my father's car.

As Aisha and I got to better know one another, I told her of the history of my friendship with Will and my aborted research into our collective past. In her mind, there was no ambiguity regarding Edward Rawlings's relationship with his "Negro woman" and one September Saturday afternoon, Aisha accompanied me to the National Archives for further research. We found the boxes of microfilm records for the Census of 1870, the first attempt of our government to provide detailed information on its newly-freed black population. After a couple of hours spooling through the documents, we finally located the records for Spotswood County. And there we found a listing for Davey Washington, age 30, and his wife Fanny, age 28. Of course, it was not uncommon for slaves to shed the surnames of their former masters and adopt the names of our founding fathers. Also listed in the household was Joseph Washington, "infant," undoubtedly my great-grandfather.

Now this information didn't prove that Fanny Washington was the same "Little Fanny," child of Edward Rawlings's "Negro woman Amy." But the chronology matched, and I knew that a slave child who reached maturity in the same antebellum location of her birth was somehow favored as so many of Virginia's slaves were sold to the cotton plantations of the deep South during those years before the war. From my research in Bluestone, I also knew that Edward Rawlings was Will's great-great-great grandfather, and now as I had reason to believe, perhaps my own ancestor as well.

That fall, Aisha and I spent every weekend together. She stayed with me Friday and Saturday nights, and we went out to movies, or "films" as I was now learning to call them, and during the day we took long walks or bike rides along the Rock Creek Parkway. Of course, Aisha had studying to do, so many hours were also devoted to reading or research at the Howard University library, where I'd sit by her side and pursue my indiscriminate program of reading begun so many years ago at St. George's. In November, Aisha invited me to go to New Jersey with her for Thanksgiving. I accepted, although I felt some residual guilt at abandoning my family since I had not had Thanksgiving with them while in college. My mother assured me it was fine; she loved Aisha, who much to my amazement, regularly exchanged letters with my parents. Besides, as my mother reminded me, I would see them at Christmas. I was excited to meet Aisha's parents. Like me, she was an only child, and we both understood the burdens and freedoms of such a dynamic. And I truly loved her, at least in the ways I best understood the meaning of that word. I know it had only been a year since my breakup with Melanie, who I also believed I had loved, but Aisha was different, and I had no trouble imagining spending my life with her.

Mr. and Mrs. Evans—or Henry and Michelle as they instructed me to call them—were genuine and accepting of me from the beginning. Their Cape Cod style home was a shrine to all things Aisha, and her soccer trophies, equestrian ribbons, and academic awards were prominently displayed with dozens of photographs from her childhood, teenage, and collegiate years. Henry and Michelle also collected African art and masks, small statues, and other objects were incongruously exhibited throughout this suburban dwelling. All in all it was a great weekend. Henry and Michelle loved their daughter, who loved me. They had raised their child to be independent and confident; they trusted her judgment and they welcomed me, no questions asked.

Will called me the week after Thanksgiving to share the news of his engagement. Of course, I was happy for him because like everyone else, apparently, I thought Sara was terrific. Details of the planned summer wedding were still incomplete, but he hoped I could come. I was noncommittal over the phone because in my mind I saw myself as likely the only black person at the affair with the possible exception of Ruth, the Rawlings's maid. I did tell him a bit about Aisha, but I didn't reveal too much, my superstition dictating not to risk my present good fortune. And I certainly didn't say anything about my "family" research; I wasn't sure how Will would receive my speculations. Before hanging up, we agreed to get together over Christmas, less than a month away.

Christmas was on a Tuesday that year, and the federal government, including the Smithsonian, granted its employees a three-day holiday. I was happy to have the time off, but knew

I would miss the month-long vacations I enjoyed in college, especially considering that Aisha was returning to New Jersey for an extended break between semesters. It would be our first prolonged separation since we had met, and I was already missing her by Saturday when I boarded the Trailways bus that took me to Richmond where my father picked me up. Though only a two hour ride, I remember that bus trip on a gray, cold day as gloomy and bereft of holiday spirit. The vehicle was crowded with old ladies off to visit grandchildren, soldiers on leave, and the requisite crying baby. Everyone seemed sad and distracted, and I vowed to myself that I would buy a car as soon as I could, despite the expense and inconvenience of parking in Washington.

Of course, it was great to see Daddy, who looked even more fit than he had during his visit in August. On the drive home, he asked me lots of questions about my job, and, not surprisingly, Aisha. That night, we enjoyed a quiet evening at home decorating the tree, and on Sunday morning I went to a sparsely-attended service at the St. George's chapel. That afternoon, Daddy and I turned on the TV and watched the Miami Dolphins beat the Cincinnati Bengals in the divisional playoffs en route to their second consecutive Super Bowl Championship.

Monday, Christmas Eve, my parents invited Dr. and Mrs. Lewis, Regina and Steven to our home for dinner. There was ham (Daddy was allowed only a small portion), mashed potatoes, green bean casserole, salad, and rolls. The Lewises brought dessert, a tasty, if somewhat misshapened cocoanut cake concocted by Regina. Of course, it was great to see Regina, who regaled us with tales of the obstreperous fourth-graders in her charge, and Steven, though reserved, related the exploits of his high school biology students. I made obligatory comments about my own work, but the conversation picked up when Mama introduced the subject of Aisha. The Lewises, especially

Regina, were eager to learn more, which made me miss Aisha desperately. When the Lewises left about nine o'clock, I called Aisha at her home in New Jersey. Henry answered the phone, and I wished him a Merry Christmas, and Michelle, too, when he put her on the line. Aisha and I talked for fifteen minutes or so, but her disembodied voice left me feeling morose. We exchanged "I love you"s, and she reminded me that we would see each other in two weeks and she promised to call the next day. I helped Daddy dry and put away the dishes after which he and Mama set out cookies and milk for Santa Claus. It was almost 11:00, and as my parents headed off to bed, they cautioned me not to stay up too late. But I knew sleep would be elusive, what with thoughts of Aisha lingering in my mind, and grabbing my tweed jacket still draped on the back of the dining room chair, I quietly slipped out the front door. It was a cold, clear night, and I saw my breath puffing in rhythm with my stride as I walked down the main drive of the campus. I had no destination in mind, just a desire to clear my head and fill my lungs, but I turned left towards town when I passed through the gates of the college. Fifty yards down the street, I saw cars parked in the small lot adjacent to Emmanuel Episcopal Church and light shown through the darkened stain-glass windows. I paused outside the red front door where I made out the last notes of "Hark! The Herald Angels Sing."

I'm not sure what prompted me to do what I did next. I know I was missing Aisha, and maybe I was feeling the need for spiritual sustenance on this, the holiest of nights. But before I could stop myself, I quietly opened the door and found myself at the rear of the still-standing congregation as the organist launched into "Angels We Have Heard on High." No one seemed to notice me, or if they did, they were perhaps, glassy-eyed at this late hour from after dinner drinks and didn't care. I scanned the full pews and located the Rawlings family. Will's parents and grandmother sat together with Jack and a young woman unknown to me, but who I assumed to be Jack's girlfriend or fiancée. Behind them sat Cathy, Will, and to my surprised delight, Sara. During the last verse of the hymn, I walked quickly down the aisle and sidled into the pew next to Will. He raised his eyebrows in surprise, but scooched over a bit and held the hymnal so I could see. Sara smiled at me, and as we all sat down, Mr. Rawlings glanced back at me and nodded.

It was a lovely, familiar service. The reading, from Luke, recounted the timeless story of Mary and Joseph's journey to Bethlehem, and the Christ child's birth in a stable because there had been no room in the inn. And in his homily, the aged Dr. Taylor focused on the arrival of the wise men, bearing gifts for the babe in swaddling clothes, the savior of the world. More hymns followed, and during the passing of the peace, I exchanged handshakes with Will and his family. And even George Turner stepped across the aisle to intone "the peace of the Lord."

The ushers passed out candles for the final hymn, "Silent Night," and as the sexton turned off the lights, two acolytes walked down the center aisle lighting the candles of the persons at the end of each pew. When my candle was lit, I touched it to Will's, and he passed the flame on to Sara. There was no organ playing as the choir began softly singing, and kneeling, we all joined in:

Silent night, holy night,
All is calm, all is bright,
Round yon virgin, mother and child,
Holy infant, so tender and mild,
Sleep in heavenly peace,
Sleep in heavenly peace.

During the final verse, Sara handed her candle to Cathy and reaching her left hand across Will, took my hand in her own while cradling Will's in her right. We blew out our candles at the conclusion of the hymn, and as Sara released our hands, I glanced at my watch. It was 12:01—Christmas Day.

About the Author

Proal Heartwell is the co-founder and co-director of Village School, a middle school for girls in Charlottesville, Virginia. He is the author of Goronwy and Me: A Narrative of Two Lives.

Made in the USA
Lexington, KY
22 November 2014